Caeia March was born on the Isle of Man in 1946 and grew up in industrial South Yorkshire. She went to London University in 1964 and graduated in Social Sciences. She has published poetry, short stories and non-fiction articles, but is best known for her novels, all published by The Women's Press – *Three Ply Yarn* (1986), *The Hide and Seek Files* (1988), *Fire! Fire!* (1991), *Reflections* (1995), and *Between the Worlds* (1996). She is also the editor of a collection of women's writing on myalgic encephalomyelitis and chronic fatigue syndrome, *Knowing ME* (The Women's Press, 1998). Caeia March has two sons, both in their twenties. Having lived in Cornwall for almost ten years, she has recently returned to Yorkshire where she intends to make her home for the foreseeable future.

CAEIA
MARCH

Spinsters' Rock

First published by The Women's Press Ltd, 1999
A member of the Namara Group
34 Great Sutton Street, London EC1V 0LQ

Where the words 'she changes everything she touches; and everything she
touches changes,' appear in the text, they are believed to have originated
in a poem by Starhawk.

British Library Cataloguing-in-Publication Data
A catalogue record for this book is available from the British Library.

ISBN 0 7043 4541 2

Typeset in Bembo 11/13pt by FSH Ltd, London
Printed and bound in Great Britain by Cox & Wyman Ltd, Reading,
Berkshire

Acknowledgements

I am very grateful to Martha Street and Penny Holland respectively, for their invaluable contributions to the understanding of, and research on, women in prison for this novel.

I would also like to thank my sons, my family in Yorkshire, and all the friends who have helped me with my recent move.

The lives of many lesbians in West Yorkshire are much enhanced by the organisation known as NOLN – the Northern Older Lesbian Network. It was a wonderful experience for me to arrive in a new city and find so many activities going on there. Thank you all for the work involved.

Last but not least, thank you to the many readers who have written to me since the publication of *Three Ply Yarn*, expressing enjoyment of that novel. Some readers asked whether I would ever meet up again with Deanne, Lotte and Esther (not forgetting Nell, of course!), and would I write about what had happened to them since the early eighties. It has been very interesting for me to revisit these 'old friends', and I have a feeling I may wish to return in years to come . . .

Book 1

Deanne
Summer, 1997

It was midsummer, ten years ago. We were driving back from friends in Crawley after a happy weekend. It was the Sunday, the day after the summer solstice, quite late, about ninish. Such a pretty evening and the sky was still light. We were in no hurry, ambling home to Brighton, a new route along the back lanes, when we saw the house: a pair of workers' cottages, rather ramshackle, set in a massive garden. Completely overgrown. The roof was tattered, with some tiles askew and the others obviously in need of attention. Out front there was a charred tree which looked as if it had been struck by lightning.

Lotte, who was behind the wheel, slowed the car, glanced sideways at me, and pulled over to the opposite verge so we could get a better view. Then she leaned over to me, patted my knee, and said, 'They've put up a For Sale sign. Come on, let's take a look.' She seemed to know exactly what I was thinking.

Dreams can be dangerous. Sometimes we try to forget them; to push them away. But they have a life of their own, such dreams, and will not remain submerged for ever. Ghost-like, they stealthily filter into the present, tapping us on the shoulder when we least expect it.

Into my mind came the image of my small house in Coombebury where I had made a home for Dora's daughter, Izzie, after Dora died. I had made a garden for Izzie and me, with colour all the year round and a plot of soil only six feet wide out front, covered in tiny blue flowers. I loved that house. I had even made a balcony garden there on the roof above the bathroom, so desperate was I to plant and grow beautiful things.

So I stepped out of the car, allowing the suppressed ghosts of need and want to touch me as I crossed the road, following Lotte.

The wooden gate was hanging off its hinges. We pushed it open and stepped into a forgotten garden, where someone had once planted roses and foxgloves, whose seed heads could now be seen, among tall unruly grasses which grew there in abundance. Holding hands, we began to wander like excited children, our feet searching for the centre of hidden pathways, our heads stooping under overhanging branches.

Since that evening, I have been to visit the famous Heligan Gardens in the West Country. There, in the early nineties, two men discovered a Victorian garden that had fallen asleep after the First World War, and they initiated a renovation project that became an inspiration for thousands of visitors. But when we stood in the neglected garden in Sussex on that special midsummer's evening, Heligan was still sleeping.

We were also somewhat like sleepwalkers as we wound our way round the jungle into an orchard. To us it seemed that the pair of cottages and surrounding garden had a slumbering quality, almost magical; a blend of mystery spiced with a hint of adventure. We found clematis and honeysuckle running rampant and some mistletoe had been grafted onto the oldest apple tree.

I'm a practical sort of person, not one to get caught up in fantasies. I like reality, for that is where life goes on each day. You get up and get ready for work – in my case a hotel in Brighton. You do a good job, bring home your pay packet, plan your holidays and simply get on with it. I never have gone in much for fantasies because, well, by definition, they aren't accessible.

But there is a difference between dreams and fantasies. I know that it is possible to dream about changes and to make those changes happen. That's the difference.

I stood there, in an acre of dereliction, and felt deeply connected to the place, as if the people who used to live there were watching me, hoping that I would set to work with secateurs and border forks, freeing up the cornflowers and discovering the cranesbills. Besides, I wasn't the first person to

4

understand that you have to dream something before you can make it happen. When Isobel dreamed of getting her A Levels and becoming an engineer, as a young bright teenager, the only black girl in Coombebury Grammar, she had told me that her inspiration was Martin Luther King, because he said, 'I have a dream.'

Isobel made her dream happen. She now worked as an engineer specialising in water-borne diseases in Africa, for the World Health Organisation. Her letters stood, in fat airmail envelopes with stunning stamps, on top of the fridge in our kitchen in Brighton.

And me? I stood in a quiet English landscape, on the rolling South Downs, thousands of miles from Isobel, wondering 'What would it take to transform this wilderness into a garden?' Dare I dream? And could I make that dream reality?

The house was empty, and the windows were cobwebbed. Rambler roses were falling off their trellises, and thistles had seeded everywhere. Round the side was an old outhouse and decrepit conservatory, and, through an archway, we found a disused vegetable garden with a woodframed greenhouse where a grape-vine was running amok, growing up through holes in the glass.

Lotte understood how much this would mean to me. By that summer of 1987 we'd been lovers for ten years. We knew exactly what the other was feeling. We could tell from the slight shift of a shoulder, or a hint of a change of tone. I was fifty-five. She was thirty-nine. We were both working full time in decent jobs, not highly paid. We didn't have degrees and stuff, but we were good workers with years of experience. And she knew how much I wanted that garden.

Lotte
Summer, 1987

Funny things, dreams. I suppose it was because Dee had such a strong feeling about the tumbledown cottages, such a need in her to move there, a longing for that place, that I started to think about my own dreams – what did I want, and where was my life taking me?

I knew I was happy. Not everybody knows that, and it's quite something. I'd been a very happy kid growing up in Densley with Mum, who worked on the buses, and my sister Essie, and Grammaclegg, Mum's mum who we lived with after Grandad died. Sometimes I'd be out playing in the yard, and I'd look up and see the washing flapping against a summer sky and I'd think, 'I like being here, I like being Lotte Clegg. I'm alive and I'm happy.'

When I was a young lass growing up in Yorkshire, all I ever wanted was a home and children of my own. I'd married James Slomner to make that dream come true but it turned into a nightmare, and I didn't have any children. I heard years after I'd left James that he remarried – some other poor rabbit to bully. But my bruises, physical and emotional, had healed by then and I lived first in Coombebury with Dee and then all these years in Brighton. I was happy at work as well because I was now an experienced legal secretary with French and English, so the work was varied and interesting. I lacked for nothing. I was devoted to Dee, and if I could help Dee make *her* dream come true, then I would.

It was a couple of nights after we'd found the house, and we'd been turning ourselves inside out trying to think of how to buy it, when I had a terrifying dream. It was so real I woke up shaking. I crept out of bed, and went downstairs to make some tea.

I sat there in the kitchen, my head spinning with the violent images. I'd dreamt of a young woman, Gail, the niece of our friend Stuart. In my dream, she'd been standing in a white room with her mother, Caroline. Caroline was shouting obscenities at her daughter, and Gail was sobbing and holding her head. There was blood – blood on her fingers. There was also someone hanging around in the background, and I don't know what it was about the figure, but it gave me a deep sense of discomfort. I shuddered. Wide awake, I could still feel the tension and emotion of the dream.

I felt like calling Stuart, but it was three in the morning and he wouldn't be best pleased. But I couldn't sleep either, so I paced up and down waiting for dawn and the seagulls' cries over Brighton.

We'd known Gail since she was a baby – a lovely kiddie, now a young woman of almost seventeen. She'd always been quiet, not very confident, but was very much loved by Stuart who took her under his wing and offered her an apprenticeship as a carpenter and general builder.

Six o'clock came. Six thirty. Seven. I knew Stuart rose early, so I phoned him.

'Hi. It's me, Lotte.'

'Hello, Lotts. This is a surprise! More about the old house, is it? Emergency? I thought you were seeing the bank today?'

'We are. I've had a terrible dream.'

'A dream? You're phoning me at seven about a dream?' There was a silence. 'This isn't like you. What's the matter?'

'I dunno. It's not the house,' I stammered. 'It was Gail. It was awful . . . Caroline was shouting the odds. It was awful. Just awful. I've been up since three. I . . . well . . .' I trailed off feeling very silly, now. I sounded silly. Reading too many magazines . . .

'Look, Lotte, it's all right. You're probably overwrought with all the excitement – it's a big project, that house. Gail'll be in to work in an hour or so. We're off on this early job, over Southampton way. I'll check it out, okay?'

'All right. Thanks. I'm sorry. I know it sounds right daft. But it was so real. I never dream like that. It was our Essie who used to have vivid dreams. Not me. I sleep like a log usually. I didn't know what to do.'

'Don't worry. Have some breakfast. Talk to Dee when she wakes up – I expect she's still out like a light.'

'Yes. 'Spect so. I didn't wake her. We've a busy day. We've the morning off to see about the money…surveyors…house…I know I'm being daft. But, thanks anyway.'

'That's fine. I'll ring you later.'

'Thanks. Bye.'

Deanne
Summer, 1987

We had to set aside our concern over Gail, after Lotte's dramatic dream, and spent the morning trying every which way to arrange a mortgage and then talking to lettings agencies about renting out our house. We were told it would be easy, because Brighton is a university town and there are always folks wanting to rent.

I'd been saving for years without really knowing why. I could've gone part time, but I liked my job at the hotel and had been doing hotel work for as long as I could remember. It began when Dora and I were young girls running away together from Mereford, in Dorset, where we had been evacuated during the war. When the war was over, the Bronnester Hotel in Coombebury had taken us in as chambermaids, no questions asked, which was just as well because we were under age. Later I became the receptionist, and my work there saved my sanity, giving me enough money to house Izzie and myself at 23 Station Road.

Now, in Brighton, living with Lotte, I was working for the Cavendish Hotel in middle management. Lotte and I both fitted well into our different jobs, and we considered ourselves very lucky. We both came from very poor families, hers in the north, mine in Rotherhithe. We were unwilling to give up our paid employment in case we toppled off the high wire and dropped down into the ring with no safety net.

So what was I up to, dreaming of a pair of ruined cottages? We lived a good life in Brighton, enough good friends, and plenty of dancing, which was our favourite pastime. We had a holiday in the sun each September on a Greek island. I could afford my expensive colour pencils and my painting things and the occasional week's residential course. It was Lotte who persuaded me to go on the first one, and made me stop calling my drawing 'doodling'.

'Don't undervalue yourself, I won't have it. Do you hear me, Dee?'

She made me laugh. After leaving James she was determined that no woman she came across would have low self-esteem or a low self-image, as she put it. She read all the books after she first came out. Her 'thing' was pop psychology. She was wonderful, coming alive, and I loved her. I've always loved her. She's the best thing that ever happened to me – after Isobel, that is. But a surrogate daughter and a lover, that's different anyway. And then there's my lifelong friend, Nell.

But underneath it all, there was always a dream which never quite faded away. It began during my time with Dora and Nell as evacuees. I think that it was the same Penny Acre Farm, in Mereford, that set up the longing; the inner dream of a place in the country, with a garden, and a view of the hills and valleys.

The farm was at the end of a long lane. I'd always said the houses were like square stone beads on a string. The river Mere ran across the road, a brown-gold river that I can still see in my mind's eye as clearly as when I was twelve years old. Me, Dora and Nell, paddling in the ford. I could draw and paint it now from memory, every whisker on every watervole, and each vein of each new leaf, not a single line blurred by the passing of time.

So, I knew from the moment we saw the For Sale sign that those two cottages had to be mine.

The financial side of things was what worried me and kept me awake at night. No one we know makes much money. We have two wealthy friends called Viv and Amy, who don't have to work, but everyone else we know works full time, and we didn't have any inheritance to fall back on. No sudden deaths of old aunties with the odd £5000. No emeralds discovered in battered leather travelling trunks in forgotten attics. But between us, by now, Lotte and I had some building skills, and I had Stuart, a gay friend, my best and longest friend besides Nell, to help me. With his practical support and advice, I felt we could take on the adventure. Well, I hoped so.

If I had thought there was a God to pray to, or anyone out there on our team, I'd have prayed. But there had been no God since my parents both died, one after the other, during the war. And any remnants of belief vanished when Dora was taken into a mental hospital and took fourteen years to die, by which time they had cooked her brain to cinders.

There was no God to pray to. But I no longer needed one. My dreams were very human ones – a little piece of paradise on earth; a calm and loving home for Lotte and myself. I wanted that place more than anything I'd wanted since the day I had first met Lotte.

Lotte
Summer, 1987

When Stuart phoned that evening to reassure us that Gail was all right, he didn't quite succeed. Stuart never was a man of many words – well, not on the phone, anyway. He was the sort who preferred to relax with a bottle of wine, face to face, and then he could go on for hours. Still, he seemed more edgy than usual and the pauses, when he hesitated, seemed much too significant. We felt that he was keeping something back. All he would say was that my dramatic dream had been surprisingly accurate – there'd been one hell of a row at home, and Gail was staying with him for a while.

The next few days were spent waiting to find tenants for our house, and marking time till the surveyor's report. Dee and I both reverted to our normal routines. But my sleep pattern had been broken by my nightmare about Gail, and a series of disturbing dreams began which disconcerted me, making me feel unstable.

I dreamed several times about James and the early years of our marriage when he had started to hit me, and to refuse to allow me to get pregnant, as if he didn't want to share me with anyone else. At first he wasn't that obvious about his intentions. He used to fob me off with tales about the mortgage and getting us better placed to have a large nursery and such like.

Some of the dream sequences were blurred and in them I seemed to be wandering through my past, looking for someone. These dreams were desolate and filled with an intense loneliness. I suppose I hadn't found much warmth and kindness after I left Mum and Densley. Mum was a kind woman. I learned how to give and receive love from her. I knew what love was, *and* what love wasn't. It wasn't making bruises on someone else's body. It wasn't keeping someone prisoner without their own needs being met. It wasn't fussing about appearance and making someone nervous about how they looked.

Each time I woke from a dream, I'd reach out a toe to touch Dee's foot and would take comfort from her sleeping beside me. I lay in the dark reliving all the long years of trying to come to terms with my marriage and all the hurt it had caused me. But then I'd think about Dee's dream house and how we would refurbish it, and what our plans and hopes were, and I knew that was love.

Someone once said to me, 'Lotte, are you a lesbian because of James?'

I laughed aloud. 'James? What has James got to do with lesbians?'

'Well, because you hated him and wouldn't go back to men.'

'For a start I don't hate men – I work with men in the office and I get on fine with them. I'm a lesbian because of love, not hate. I'm a lesbian because I love myself now and it's the best thing for me. I'm a lesbian because if I had daughters I'd like them to be lesbians if it would make them as happy as I am.'

That's the test I always think: 'Would you want your daughter to be one?'

If you can't say yes to that simple question, then perhaps you haven't understood about lesbians, and how it can feel to hold a beautiful woman in your arms and look into her eyes and make love with her and her with you. And maybe you haven't silenced those old prejudices deep inside you.

The series of dreams brought me up against my own reality, and my lost dreams of having children. But I didn't yearn for kids any more. Besides, my life hadn't been totally devoid of them because being lovers with Dee meant I'd met Gail, and had been able to watch her growing up.

I didn't have any more dreams about Gail, but I thought about her a lot. She seemed to be a gentle presence there, at the back of my mind.

Otherwise things went on fairly much as normal. The first

mortgage surveyor's report came quickly and shocked us with the amount of work required. We knew by then that the main mortgage giants wouldn't touch us, so we went to a broker that Stuart recommended – a gay friend of his, based in Brighton. He liked us, said we had verve (whatever that was), and would try to help. We put in an offer but it was rejected; that gave us goosebumps. Did we dare meet what the vendors wanted? And if we didn't, would we lose the cottages? Just the small matter of money...

The following Sunday, we decided to visit the place again. We asked Stuart if he would come and cast a financial eye over the property, this time with the surveyor's report in his hand, and his builder's experience in mind. Supposing we managed to raise the mortgage, could we afford to do all the necessary work? We'd made a new offer subject to surveys and contract, and were biting our nails while waiting for the vendors' response.

Dee and I had prepared vegetables, dips and a salad, and had packed the food carefully into a cooler chest, with fresh, crusty bread. It was a beautiful day, and we decided to eat the picnic in the garden of the old house.

The talk over lunch was bright and cheerful, full of our plans for the renovations. Dee and I wanted to knock the two cottages into one house, so that there would be plenty of room for visitors. We'd also decided on a name for the house – Mere Cottage. However, it was clear that Stuart was waiting to tell us something, and the conversation soon turned to the subject of Gail and my disturbing dream.

'It's not easy being a single parent, like Caroline, I suppose,' he began.

Dee shook her head sympathetically, remembering her years with Izzie.

'I'm trying to understand Caroline – after all, she's my sister – but it's hard. Especially when I see how much she's upset Gail.'

'How is she, then?'

'Very badly shaken up by the row. She doesn't want to go home.'

'So what really went on?' I asked. 'I mean, I thought they got

14

on well most of the time. That's why the dream was so shocking. Caroline was really letting rip.'

'I know. And Gail fell over, hurt her head. She won't say much about it. Just that she won't go back.'

'Fell and hurt her head? That's a bit of an old chestnut!'

'I know. But she won't talk about it. I took her to casualty, but she kept insisting that she'd just slipped. The thing is, she hit her head hard, just above her ear, against the corner of the worktop. The doctors think she might've damaged her ear. They have to do some tests.'

'That must've been some row. What was it about?'

'She's keeping schtum. Won't say a word.' Stuart shifted, then added, 'But there is something I want to run by you ...'

'That sounds ominous.' Dee smiled. 'I know you, you've got something up your sleeve.'

'Up Gail's sleeve, actually. It's her idea.'

We waited for Stuart to get on with it. Dee knew him very well. There was no use trying to rush him into talking. One never could, with Stuart.

He took a sip of his wine, looking nervously from me to Dee and back again, then asked, 'Would you be willing to take Gail in, let her live with you?' There was silence. I realised that both Dee and Stuart were looking at me, as if this were my decision alone. Dee was one of Stuart's oldest friends and she'd always regarded him as family. He'd also been a great support to her, so he probably knew she would always do whatever she could to help him.

As for me, well, it was a bit of a shock, but not an unpleasant one. I knew that having Gail live with us wouldn't be like having a child of my own, but I didn't want or need to dream about having children any more. Now having let go of my dream, here was an unexpected gift to replace it. I've heard the saying many times, that if you really let go of something, it is only then that it can come back to you. But this was my first deep experience of its truth. To be an older friend to Gail, who was young and obviously very vulnerable, to be able to provide warmth and security to someone who needed it so desperately, seemed a beautiful and heartwarming opportunity. A real gift.

15

There was something else going on in my mind, as well. One of the reasons I had stayed with James long after I 'should' have left was that I had nowhere to go. I didn't know what my dramatic dream about Gail actually meant, but I knew that it was significant. I was sure that Gail had left behind some sort of domestic violence. Call it instinct, intuition, or women's hidden knowledge. I don't mind what anyone calls it, but it was real to me. The dream sequence and now Stuart sitting with us telling us that Gail needed a home, brought back all my memories of the times I had needed somewhere to go. I didn't know what Gail was running from, but I did know that she was running from something.

'We need time to think about this, do we Lotte?' Dee asked, kindly. I loved her even more in that instant. Her first reaction would have been to say yes to Stuart immediately. But she had this capacity, always, to be gracious about my needs and not dump hers on me.

'Gail is very welcome in our home, in Brighton if need be, but especially here if we can swing this one, eh Dee?'

'Thank you, Lotte. Are you sure?' Dee reached out a hand to grab mine and her other to hold Stuart's. We sat without speaking, aware of three friends, and beginnings.

Stuart sighed with relief. He told us that he'd been very tense, and worried about Gail's future, and he'd been bottling it up. After all, Gail couldn't stay in his place for ever, isolated from other women, could she?

I thought about that. You don't fall against a worktop when your mother is yelling at you, then say absolutely nothing about it, unless there is much, much more going on. And you don't simply refuse to go back to all that is familiar, and thereby render yourself homeless, unless that situation is intolerable, do you? Perhaps, living with Dee and me, Gail might begin to open up, trust us enough to tell the whole story. That's what I hoped, anyway.

Stuart said, 'Thank you both. Love you both. Come on, let's see what the damage is on this heap of decay. We'll have our work cut out, all of us, that's for certain. You know that don't you?'

'Think of it all as an adventure,' said Dee. And that shut him up.

Gail
Diary, Summer, 1987

I can't tell Stuart. I can't tell anyone. I have to go forward in my life and get on with it. I can't forgive Mum for the things she said...or for the things she did. People have to say sorry before you can forgive them. But how can I forgive her when I know she's never wanted me? Being in the world when you're not wanted, it feels cold inside.

Writing this in my diary, here at Stuart's in Coombebury. I want to try to make sense of everything. I want to know why this has happened to me. Mum says it's my own fault. What she really means is that it's my fault for being born.

They say school days are the best days of your life. Never believe that. I hated school. I was given a home tutor eventually, because they couldn't put up with my panic attacks at the school gate. I've never fitted in anywhere.

I know I'm not one of the world's beautiful people. I'm not even noticeably plain like Jane in Charlotte Brontë's novel. I'm not noticeable at all – there is nothing to distinguish me. Jane Eyre at least had dark hair, probably shining and flowing down to her waist, when she brushed it at night. They did in those days. I'm not a dark-haired beauty with dark eyes. I'm not a blonde with bright blue eyes either. Light brown hair, nondescript looks, eyes that aren't grey and aren't hazel, but somewhere in between. Middling. Ordinary. Not exactly ugly, but definitely not *wanted*.

Well, not wanted by my mum. I have known what it feels like to be loved and that's what has kept me going. Uncle Stuart and his partner, Eddie, have always shown me what love is. Kind people, hard working. I wanted to go and live with them when I was small. Some weekends when Mum was working I did stay with them and I'd be given a piece of wood to whittle, and I would make people, whole families of them. I didn't take them home. Mum wouldn't have liked them and she couldn't bear my things strewn around. I'd have had to keep them in a box. People don't belong in boxes. I didn't. Not in that box with Caroline, my mother.

I'd say I've been working with wood with Stuart since I was five – wood turning, wood engraving, wood carving. The wood is smooth and giving under my hands. I'd describe that as love. I make things with love. I heard the other day that woodworkers and carpenters have the lowest suicide rate in this country and it doesn't surprise me. Job satisfaction, I expect. Now, I have a skill that pleases people and there is so much more to learn. Stuart has always praised me for my work, and he is a great teacher. He knows how to break everything down into simple steps and put them in the right sequence.

So, in all these years of pain and hurt with my mum, knowing how much she resented me and feeling her anger at me, even when she was sweet talking, I've never felt like taking my own life. It's mine and I do want to stay alive. But I did wonder if I was going to die when my head hit the worktop. They say I might be deaf as a result – hearing impaired or something.

What I thought of, dreamed of, for years, was getting away from home. But not running away. I wanted to plan it so that I could end up working for Stuart, in the trade. Then I ended up running anyway, when the crisis came.

The other people who have always shown me love are Lotte and Deanne. Stuart's with them now, looking at their old cottages. I like their lifestyle. I like how they are with one another. Not like Mum and her boyfriends, rowing and shouting. Slamming about. I was staying with them, Lotte and Deanne, once when they had a party. That was when their old friend Corrine was still alive. I called her Aunty, like the rest of them, when I was small. She used to be the singer at the Bronnester Hotel, here in town, where

Deanne started off work as a chambermaid. Deanne told me wonderful stories about the attic there. It was a thin room with only one bed so she and Dora had to snuggle up. She'd also told me about Isobel, the daughter Dora had just before she was taken away.

Three years ago, when I was fourteen, Lotte and Deanne let me go with them to scatter Corrine's ashes in the New Forest. It was autumn and I can remember the rich russet colours on the trees and the birdsong. Corrine sang beautifully, even as an old woman, and she would've loved that simple ceremony in the forest. I did. I cried buckets, and Stuart gave me his large white handkerchief. I walked home holding Lotte's hand and it felt like being with a real family, one that wants you.

There were two other old women there, called Vivienne and Amy, but no one used their names. Everyone always called them after the museum, the V&A. I asked Lotte why and she explained that the museum in London is stuffed full of antiques, just like the house the two of them own out in the back of beyond. They have to take a lot of teasing, but they are also very kind. We went on to their place, the Froggery, near Dorchester, that weekend for supper, and stayed overnight. I always wrote down in my diary about the people who were kind, because I never knew kindness at home.

Later.

I walk along the cliffs looking out to the horizon, a deep blue line between the sky and the sea. I make my way down the zigzag path to the shore, then along the edge of the waves, watching the last few holidaymakers packing up ready for their evening meal. Soon I have the beach almost to myself. I watch the sun shimmering on the waves and I dream of going to live in that falling apart place with Lotte and Deanne. It would be a peaceful life and I would work like a dog to help them rebuild it, to repay their kindness – if only they will take me in and give me the chance of a new home. I throw pebbles into the sea, making wishes as if I were only five or six years old, a child again. But I am no longer a child, not after everything I have been through. What I need now is a new life.

When I return home, Eddie tells me Stuart has rung.

They said, Yes.

Deanne
October, 1987

We had thought of renting out our Brighton house because we hadn't expected to get a buyer. We were afraid that if we waited and were caught up in a chain, we might lose the pair of cottages. However, it became obvious to us that raising the necessary mortgage on a property in need of so much repair was going to prove very difficult indeed.

Gail came to live with us during August in Brighton, bringing with her a chest of drawers that she was making. On good days she worked in our back yard, moving into the kitchen in the basement if it rained. She was very quiet, quite closed, and liked to spend the evenings in her room listening to music. Slowly we began to get used to her, and her to us. She never spoke about her mother or the row they'd had, but Lotte and I knew she just needed her own time and space. Meanwhile the waiting around for news of the cottages was nearly driving us all crazy.

Then, one morning before I left for work, the broker rang us asking if we could meet him during our lunch hour. It might be in our interest, he said, to hear what he had to say.

'Come in, sit down both of you. Tea?'

We shook our heads, because time was short.

'I have a possible buyer for your house here in Brighton.'

'A *buyer*?'

'Two friends of mine, Stephen and Charles – they own an antique business in the Lanes. Money no object.' He paused looking sadly but whimsically from one to the other of us. 'Regrettably, they are in something of a crisis. Stephen has fallen

21

for someone else. Sad business; they've been together twelve years.'

We waited. We couldn't think of anything to say. We didn't know whether to look sympathetic or hopeful, so we both just tried to stay calm, maintain composure. I heard myself take a huge deep breath. Said nothing.

Our broker continued, 'Charles needs somewhere to live, a place of his own and very quickly. He wants to stay in Brighton, because all his friends are here. He has family money. It'd be cash. Your mortgage worries would be over.'

'Bang goes your commission?' asked Lotte.

'Mortgaging those cottages for the size of loan you wanted was looking rather shaky, as well you know. But with the capital from your house as deposit, we're not looking at raising so much, are we?'

We bobbed our heads like a pair of nodding dogs. Both of us were rendered speechless, which takes some doing.

'So, what do you think?'

I turned to Lotte, who was shining.

'I can't believe it,' she began, 'I've been waking at three in the morning, trying to come up with schemes to help us. Honestly, John, I've been *so* worried. We knew you were doing your best, but it was dragging on and we couldn't bear to lose the place now. We've both been spinning rather a lot of dreams around it. I suppose people do, don't they?'

'Of course they do. Anyone would. It's a lovely place and it's only natural to set your hopes on it. I've put down some figures. House prices are currently rising very fast, as you know, and your property is worth far more than you'd have got three years ago, even. The financial people in the City think the peak will come within a year or so from now. They may be right. You would need to come down a bit for this quick sale but Charles would not rip you off. Anyway – ' John looked at his watch, ' – I realise your lunch hour is all too short, so take these sheets, and peruse them. I did a copy for each of you...'

My hand was shaking so much I could barely hold the pieces of paper he passed to me.

'Ring me tomorrow morning and we're ready to roll, if you agree to the figures and the terms. Of course, we have to take off the remainder of your present mortgage but you'd still be left with a tidy deposit, if you add it to your savings. Well done, both of you. I am sure that this is meant to be.'

'You've been wonderful, John, thank you. You've really done your best by us.'

'Any friend of Stuart's is a friend of mine. Keep it in the family, that's my motto. It couldn't happen to a nicer couple. We'll talk in the morning, all right?'

'Till tomorrow then.'

'Bye, John. Thanks again.'

We had to change the house name officially at the post office. They didn't mind. They said that people do it all the time. It was approaching the autumn equinox when we moved in, exactly eleven weeks after we'd found it.

We decided to camp out in the rooms downstairs and to have the outhouse made into our own bathroom, leading off our downstairs bedroom. The fourth room downstairs would be the sitting room; and the two kitchens out the back would be knocked into one huge farmhouse-style kitchen, complete with an Aga.

Housing is always expensive in the south of England. We weren't surprised that others had turned it down, waiting for the price to drop. But after the first offer was rejected we hadn't dared quibble in case we lost it. We used all my savings, the full price of the Brighton house, and a mortgage, which John arranged for us. But in the meantime Lotte and I had come up with a plan. Just before seeing the cottages, I'd been doing a lot of thinking about the future. I knew I wanted to do something when I retired, and Mere Cottage provided me and Lotte with the perfect opportunity. If I retired at sixty – which wasn't far off, only five years – I could run Mere Cottage as a B&B for women. That way I'd still be able to make a living and I knew I'd enjoy meeting the women who came to stay.

So Lotte and I planned that we would take our time to get the place ready, evenings and weekends, with Gail's invaluable help. Then I would open the B&B in the summer of 1992 when I retired, and Lotte would carry on with her job, which she enjoyed, and from which we would need the income. So that's how we sorted it.

I lay there that first night, with the smell of damp and the grimy paint, knowing that the roof leaked, that there was no central heating, the windows were rotten, and the vegetable plot would have challenged the women's land army, but I didn't care. Lotte was sleeping soundly beside me, Gail was happy and safe. I was home, and everything in my garden was beautiful.

Nell
October, 1987

Where there's muck, there's money. That's what I tells Beth, my neighbour here in Reeve Green. Work's dodgy right now. We've lost so many calls a week. They'll have to hooft out more than one of us. That's recession for you.

So Beth says to me, 'What'll you do, Nell? What will you *do*?'

'Well,' I says to her, 'Let's say it goes like this: I gets into Slomners tomorrer, and I gets to the lobby and they tells me I'm hoofted. They frogmarches me up to the upstairs and gives me my papers. Then they marches me back down to me desk and I has to clear me things, which is how they do it, right? Then they takes me to the front door and says goodbye to me. I goes home. I has a long long sleep. Then, next day, I goes down to the dole and I signs on. Because you know what?'

'What?' says Beth.

'When I signs on I gets me rent paid. And I gets a proportion of me council tax paid and I gets free eyes and free teeth. Then I goes back indoors and I sorts out me money. With me lump sum I pays for me two weeks intensive driving. Then I gets me car – I buys a heap of shit on wheels – and off I goes. And I becomes the yuppie cleaner.'

'A cleaner?' says Beth.

'Oh yes,' I says. 'See this hand? I've had this hand down many a toilet in my time and when I takes this hand out, the toilet's shining. Shining. Where there's muck, there's money. I already do Cyril's. A nice little earner. But I can't get to the others because I can't drive. So if this office throws me out, that's what I am going to do. That or fostering. I like kids. I've always liked 'em. Him indoors, he likes kids too. We'd do it together, fostering.'

'Not another office job then Nell?'

'An office? When I leave this switchboard I am never, never, never entering another office, nor picking up another poxy phone ever again. Because there is so many arseholes on the end of those phones you just wouldn't believe it.'

Apart from that, things are fine, just fine. I told Ess, in my last letter. 'Himself,' I said, 'He's still where you last left him, lying on the floor in front of the telly, wearing a hole in my carpet. That's his function in life now, making a hole in that carpet. He's still got his two speeds, dead slow and stop, bless him. He don't do no harm and we jog along all right. His back still plays him up, that's why he can't do the buses no longer. It was killing him, really. That and the fire brigade all those years ago. It wore him out and he had his first breakdown over that. Well, him being the fire-engine driver, they have to drive through the red lights whatever. Then, if they do get it wrong and crash into someone, it's their fault. That's a no-win situation. It did his head in. They said it was stress. And his biorhythms all messed up. Eating all funny hours of the day and night. That gave him an ulcer. Shift work got his body and the red lights got his head. Never been right since, though he liked the buses. Then he went for another driving job – an ambulance driver with the old ladies, taking them home from hospital. But if the lifts weren't working he'd end up getting them in the wheelchair, up the stairs, and all. That's no good for someone with back trouble. So then he was in agony on the floor, wearing a hole in the carpet again and sadder than he was before he started the job. "Don't get old, Nell. Don't let's get old." It was awful to see him so sad.'

He's gone to Ascot today, taken a whole minibus full. Gets paid for that and it's not too bad.

I was just glad that I had my insurance from work when his disc went. He had to crawl to the toilet and sometimes he was so bad he had to pee into a bowl on the floor. To see him reduced to that . . . So I phones up the private hospital and I says what state he's in and that it's six months to his appointment on the National Health. She says to me on the phone, 'I'm so sorry Mrs Winters,

26

but we can't fit him in until Tuesday.'

'Which Tuesday would that be?' I asks.

'Oh, this Tuesday but it's four days away. I'm terribly sorry.'

'Oh, four days,' I says to her. I looks at Fred there on the carpet. He's crying, the pain is so bad.

I smiles into the phone, at the lady. She must've heard me smiling. I says, 'This Tuesday would be fine, thank you so much.'

Four days, compared to six months. That's what money can do. So I goes with him and they operate the following Sunday. That was just eight days after I phoned them for our first appointment. I takes all me insurance documents from work, and I hands them over and they read all the small print. 'That's fine Mrs Winters,' they say to me. Smiling. Everyone was smiling. 'That's fine, your spouse is insured on your work policy.'

It gets more like America every day in this country.

That's where Esther is, America. I miss her, but she needs a fresh start. She's working there now, San Francisco. Nice apartment in Oakland, with a view of the bay (they don't call them flats over there). I love her letters, all full of love and life and stories. She's writing a book for our Billie – she's into children's books in a big way. Multicultural, all sorts. That's my Ess. She cares about all that, she always has done. I miss her and San Francisco's a long, long way. But it was for the best, after everything that happened to Esther.

Esther
November, 1987

The plane touched down at Heathrow and I wasn't sure if it felt like homecoming or not. In my mind were images of the Californian redwoods: tall trees, warm fires, the shadows of dancing women weaving in and out of the trees, silhouettes of women drumming in the firelight.

I was on my way back to an uncertain future. Phoebe and I had decided to spend the next three months together, in England, house-sitting for Phoebe's mother. We had to find out what was possible for us. My heart, my body and my soul were already involved and, in a few minutes, there would be Phoebe, waiting at the airport for me.

I hadn't meant to fall in love with her. It was already causing trouble – not because Phoebe was a black woman, but because her ex-lover was Isobel Beale – and Isobel was Deanne's daughter, and my sister Lotte was Deanne's lover. So it was all too damn close.

I had certainly been excited when I heard that Phoebe and Isobel had both been invited to San Francisco to deliver research papers at a huge symposium on world health. I'd never met Phoebe and I hadn't seen Isobel for a long time. I was so looking forward to catching up with all her news, spending pleasant evenings together in the local wine bars and the cosy cafés of the Castro. For me, it had all seemed like perfect timing – it'd be a link with Dee and Lotte again, like touching base. However, my dreams of a companionable reunion with Isobel and some cheerful tour guiding were based on false assumptions about Isobel and Phoebe's tête-à-tête togetherness. As soon as they arrived it had become obvious that things were very wrong between them.

Isobel hadn't stayed long but Phoebe had a brother in San Francisco, so she decided to spend some more time there. Then she was offered some temporary lecturing work at the university.

No, it had not been an easy beginning. I had fallen in love with Phoebe while she was in the final stages of a messy break-up with Isobel and my apartment in Oakland was one of the places to which she had fled.

Every one of my friends warned me – you can't afford to fall for Phoebe. She and Izzie are two black women with a depth of shared work, politics and loving. If they are splitting up, well, surely they need time and space to make a friendship. Where's your politics gone, honey? Gee, honey, you sure know how to drop yourself in it, don't you? You mustn't start this new relationship at this time. You'll crowd them out, Ess. Don't let it happen, Ess.

But it was too late by then. Rebound or not, I knew that what Phoebe and I had was special. Maybe I was wrong, who's to say? I had to follow my heart and body, and so did she. After all, she wasn't exactly a passive spectator in all of this, was she?

I wrote to Nell, but she was horrified.

Nell and I had been writing to each other every week since my arrival in America, and usually I loved to get her letters which were very domestic – all about her washing machine, her new kitchen, and so on.

They were often funny but I also got very long, serious letters about her daughters and how they were getting on. She had always had a volatile relationship with one of them, Tracey, and recently there had been a lot of trouble. Meanwhile, I had my own guilt about not having supported Tracey when she had come to me as a young teenager seeking advice about the process of coming out. I just hadn't helped her. I had been too busy grappling with my own uncertainties around my sexuality at the time. Hardly the all-seeing, all-knowing, wise older woman. I had been working on the *Three Ply Yarn* book with Dee and Lotte and had been trying so hard to come to terms with my break-up with Christine and with my own love for women. I was not at all 'out'.

I hadn't been ready for Tracey. But I was ready for Phoebe.

'You want yer head testing, Ess,' Nell had written. 'You've really been and gone and done it this time!'

Maybe, maybe not. For once in my life I didn't care what anyone else thought. Nor if I was 'doing the right thing', being the true 'right-on' woman. I couldn't live like that any longer. I had to know if what I shared with Phoebe was real, because it was for me. She brought me abundance. New friendship when I wasn't searching. New loving when I least expected it. The warmth of her heart, the ease of our communication, the touch of her hair, the feel of her skin, the scent of her...

I see you, Phoebe, emerging wet from the shower. I lead you by your hand to our bed. We know that we need this. It is our knowledge from experience. We crave one another's touch, respond to each other's needs. My tongue skims the soft tender skin of your neck and lingers upon your breasts. I stroke the curves of your inner arms, your belly, your hips, your thighs, my palms mapping the landscape of your body. I bury my face in the deep valley between your legs and explore you, delighting you with my tongue, until you cry out my name.

Now you reach into me. I am a volcano, passionate with fire and air. You feel me calling you, welcoming your strong and loving fingers, encouraging you, until deep, in the most remote recesses of my body, you touch my centre.

Another time, in calm, reflective mood, we talk quietly, in one another's arms.

You say, 'In the centre of each of us is the "I", the one who recognises a kindred spirit, the one who knows.'

'Yes, from cognito, to know, to understand.'

You say, 'And to see. In our foreheads we have a third eye, so that we can become women of vision, women who see with our minds. In ancient Africa to know was to see, and all knowledge came from the womb.'

'Like those female figurines of old Europe, with an eye drawn on their bellies.'

You say, 'Yes. Womb and eye – the womb-eye synthesis.'

'In old England, all knowledge came from our vulvas. A cunning woman was one who was wise. Cunnit was the verb to know. Sexuality and spirituality combined.'

You desire me again, and the 'I' in me answers completely.

Now, here I am, making my way through customs, moving towards you again. And my mind recalls with clarity, and my body with joy, every moment of pleasure and loving with you.

Then there Phoebe was, her eyes searching along the lines of us as we came through customs and out into the airport foyer. She'd had her hair cut. Very, very short so that it showed off the beauty of her head and neck. She wore tiny gold axes in her ears, and her very dark skin and black eyes were as stunning and familiar as ever.

'You're here. I love you, Ess.'

'I've missed you, Phee. I love you too.'

We held each other close, in front of everyone, greeting like two long lost friends. Which we were, in a way.

'I've a gift for you from Matt,' I said. 'He sends his love, they all do.'

'My baby brother.' She laughed. 'Okay, let's help you with all this stuff.'

'You sure it's all right for me to stay at your mum's house, with you?'

'It's time, Ess. Mum knows the score. She likes to be on the inside, that's what Mum needs.'

'Really?'

'Yes, really. She's not one to judge. It's not her style. I had a letter from Lagos this morning, actually. She's having a wonderful time. It's her first holiday for twelve years.'

'I'm glad for her. Must be marvellous to be back with all her family. Okay then. So long as you're sure, Phee.'

She grinned at me and wrinkled her nose in that familiar endearing gesture that I had come to know and love. Her eyes were so warm, deep, happy to be with me.

*

I fell silent as we hauled all the baggage down escalators and on to the tube. I was thinking of Phoebe's mum back in Nigeria after a long time away from there, and it led me naturally to my own family, and my recent conversation with my sister, Lotte.

'I know it's expensive to phone international but I so needed to hear your voice, Lotte. I'll be home soon. It'll be so good to see you again.'

'You, too, Essie. I'm not much of a letter writer, am I?'

'You're not wrong about that, Lotts. But anyway it's not the same as face to face, is it?'

I was thinking about the long rift between us when Lotte first got married. I'd seen through James in a second and I hated the way he treated my sister. Then, just when we'd finally managed to reconnect and sort out our differences, my life had fallen apart. I couldn't live near Reeve Green, or the school. I just had to get away.

'San Francisco has been kind to me. I wrote to Nell, last week, but I haven't phoned her yet, it's all been so hectic,' I said.

'Well it would be, you falling for Izzie's lover.' She paused, then said, in her broadest Densley accent, 'Jesus wept, Esther Clegg, you don't half jump in the deep end, my girl.'

'That was a brilliant imitation of our mum! How do you do it, Lotte?'

We both laughed.

Lotte continued, 'When you talk to Nell do give her our love. She likes being a granny – Sally's living at home with the baby. Things are working out okay for her now. But there's some problem with Tracey – there always are problems with Tracey...'

'Last time Nell wrote, Tracey was working down the market.'

'She still is, but Nell is convinced there's drugs going on at the flat. She's worried sick about who Tracey's friends are these days.'

'Nell always was very anti-drugs. She can't abide smoking, not anything, even pot. I mean, I still think pot ought to be legalised.'

'Go easy on her, Essie. Nell is truly frantic about Tracey. I know they're all on the weed in California, and I know all the young ones smoke it here, but I don't think Nell's talking about pot –

tread very lightly, Essie, or she'll have a turn. She is terrified. Anyway I ought to go – this is costing you a fortune and I'll see you when you get back. But there is just one thing, Ess?'

'Don't like the sound of this . . .'

'Yes, I know. It's, uhm, I, er . . . I don't think you should push it about visiting here with Phoebe. I'll come to you. I do love you, you know that, but Dee is hurting very badly for Izzie, because Izzie did not want to break up with Phoebe.'

'I didn't break them up, you know. I just happened to fall in love with Phoebe when their relationship was in its death throes. There are no rules about falling in love.'

'That's where you're wrong, Ess. There *are* rules and sometimes they get broken. Doesn't stop me loving you, Ess. But I live here with Dee and I cannot bear to hurt her. I will not hurt her. Not even for you. Please, don't ask me to.'

'You'll come to London?'

'Of course I will.'

'Thank you. See you in London then. Love you lots, Lotts.'

She laughed at the old reminder of our Densley childhood.

'Love you Essie, Sissie.'

The other woman I longed to meet again was Laura who had been my friend through our teenage years, in the north.

The Randalls had moved in next door to us in Densley, the first black family in our very white area. My Grammaclegg hadn't been best pleased. 'I don't want you getting too close to them, our Essie.' But I had defied her on that one, deliberately and openly. Laura and I had been single-minded about getting ourselves an education. We both saw it as a one-way ticket out of Densley. We spent every minute together, closeted in her bedroom, reading, writing and talking. She had her own room and we did all our homework there, setting our chins at the future with steel-sharp determination. Our need for one another's support at Densley High was intense and our friendship had flourished. We would never now allow ourselves to lose touch. Her letters were a source of continuity and, frequently, they brought messages of hope. She had been shocked at my decision to leave Reeve Green for San Francisco. She wrote:

It's hardly a day return to Bristol from London, is it Esther? How am I going to get to see you? When am I ever going to see you again? I do understand, I know you need to get right away from everything that's happened, but isn't halfway round the world a bit excessive? I just wish you'd chosen to come here and stay with me and Joseph, that's all.

The girls miss you and send their love. Sophie has now passed her grade five clarinet, and Melody has developed an interest in computers, which has taken us all by surprise. She says that's what she wants to do as a career. I told her she's got plenty of time – after all, she's only fourteen! But she managed to persuade us to stretch the family finances to an all-singing, all-dancing state-of-the art computer. I think she sees it as only fair after all the golden guineas we shell out on Sophie's music. At least the computer is QUIET! I'm just glad that Sophie has chosen the clarinet, not the trumpet. Be grateful for small mercies!

Write soon. We miss you. There's always room for you here, don't ever forget that. Be safe and happy. But *come back* some day. Okay?

Love,
Laura

It was a long way across London and plenty of changes by tube and train. Time to absorb the nearness of Phoebe and the strange absence of the Babel Tower of languages that was the city I'd just left behind.

There, on the buses and trolleys, I'd hear Italian, Japanese, Chinese, several other East Asian tongues, Russian, all the East European languages and, of course, Spanish everywhere. These were interspersed with a vast variety of American accents, according to who the speakers were, where they had been raised and how they'd been raised. Black, white, people of colour – all had different voices speaking 'American'. I loved it. There was nowhere like it in the world.

Not that London wasn't cosmopolitan, but the ambience was different and it was a shock. I heard more than a few voices that were not speaking English and, of course, there were some Americans on the tube. But despite all this and the familiar assortment of faces and voices, London didn't have the easy flair of San Francisco – the place where I'd fallen in love with Phoebe. I had been away from London for a long time, and perhaps I didn't belong there any more – perhaps it was no longer home.

Tracey
November, 1987

I was so proud of that car. I drove it everywhere. That night I'd gone over to Vauxhall to see friends. Good friends, nice food. I had two glasses of red wine, which is more than I usually have, but I thought it'd be all right. I could've stayed over but I wanted to sleep in my own bed, not on Kelly's floor. So I set off home. It was about one in the morning.

I was tired, but I was concentrating hard. Then this black cat ran right out in front of me and I swerved. I missed it, thank God. Then the lights changed. Amber, so I stopped. I didn't know there was this cop car parked up. They'd seen me swerve but they wouldn't have seen the cat. It was black on a black road.

They breathalised me and that's how I got my ban. I was really pissed off. Fifteen months.

I'd nearly finished my ban, when Sally came round to my flat with Billie. Sally had borrowed Earl's car. Billie was crawling. Into everything.

Anyway, she was in the living room with Sally, or so I thought. I was making tea in the kitchen. There was an almighty yell and there was Billie rolling down the stairs. Over and over. Rolling down.

Sally screamed and Billie screamed. She had a bloody face. It was awful. All curled up at the foot of the stairs, bawling her eyes out.

I didn't stop to think about the ban. I just didn't think. I went on instinct. I grabbed Sally's car keys and we were in that car, dashing to casualty with me driving like a bat out of hell before you could say 'hospital'.

I was belting down Lewisham High Street when they got me. They forced me to pull over. All I could think of was Billie, screaming.

'It's the baby,' I yelled. 'It's the baby. She's fallen down the stairs.'

'Follow us,' they said. So I did. Sally rushed in with the baby and then they quizzed me. Name, address, driving licence. I thought, hell, now I've done it.

I got sent down for it. They'd caught me driving while banned. They gave me a choice – either pay a hefty fine or do twenty-eight days. Well, that was no choice for someone like me. Where was I going to get the money to pay a fine like that? So I chose to do time, but, in the end, it was only two weeks.

That was where I met Maxie. I thought she was the most beautiful dyke I'd ever seen. I was bowled over by her. I heard myself say, 'If you're ever in Lewisham, drop by and see me.' I should be so lucky. I never thought she would.

I'd been back at the flat about a month when Maxie came by. She said she didn't have anywhere to live. Could I put her up for a week or two while she got herself sorted.

I couldn't resist her. She was beautiful. Sex was wonderful. Mum went mad.

Nell
November, 1987

I didn't trust her. Not Maxie. Not from the moment I set eyes on her. I knew she was trouble. I started to keep an eye on the flat. People coming and going at all times. Trace was down the market. That's eight to five. But there was still a lot of action. So they weren't coming to see Trace.

I said to her, 'It's drugs, Trace. You want to be careful. There's bodies coming and going all hours. Connie Sandforth lives opposite. I've known Connie all my life. She's straight as a die. She says there's bodies coming and going all hours.'

'Bloody busybody. It's none of her business.'

'Drugs is everybody's business these days, Trace. You want to be careful you know.'

'I lead my life and Connie Bloody Sandforth can lead hers. She's no right spying on me.'

'I asked her to that's what.'

'You did WHAT?'

'You heard me first time, Tracey. You've already done time and you'll be doing time again you mark my words. That Maxie is trouble.'

'Don't be stupid, Mum. So, she has a puff. So what? We all do. They can't get you for having a puff. Get off my back, Mum.'

'It's more than that, Trace. I'm sure it is.'

'Oh that's wonderful, that is, Mum. The trouble with all of you is your lives are so damned small that you have to spy on us just for a bit of interest. Well just lay off, Mum. And you can tell Connie to pack it in right now.'

So I kept quiet after that but I made a few phone calls just in

38

case. I had a couple of blokes I knew from back in Dockland days that owed me a small favour or three, so I asked them to keep watch.

And after a while I was certain I was right.

But I couldn't let on that I'd got friends staking out the place. She'd have cut me out of her life and I didn't want that. Not after letting her down so badly when she first came out. She had left home because I failed her. I've failed my Trace so many times. I didn't want to fail her now. But I kept watch, when I could, just the same.

Gail

December, 1987

I'd been living at Mere Cottage all through the autumn, and the memories of the summer were gradually loosening their grip. I felt a new energy surging inside me as I threw myself into the work on the house. For the first time in a long while I felt safe. Dee and Lotte provided me with all the security I needed at that point, but they also knew when to give me space. I was learning to trust again. Despite this, I did feel as if I was always holding part of myself back from them. They never pushed me for details on why I'd left home, and I never told them.

When I first moved into the house in Brighton, I was glad to just be. I wanted to settle down – emotionally, that is. I knew it would take time for me to overcome everything that had happened to me when I was little, and more recently. But I also realised that hiding something isn't dealing with it, and as the winter drew on, I decided I wanted to start the New Year with a clean slate. Not that I was the one to blame – I'd distanced myself from my mother enough to realise that now. But I did want to open up more with Lotte and Deanne so that I could leave the past behind and just get on with my life. And I had so much to tell them.

The bombshell that hit lesbians and gay men just before Christmas was that the government published a bill about local councils and what they could spend their money on. There was a clause in it that no one had expected – at that time, when it was first published, it was Clause 14. It went round the lesbian and gay networks like a Chinese whisper, little bits added or subtracted here and there, but people were soon phoning friends for proper

40

information. In the world that Dee and Lotte lived in there was always someone who knew something, or knew who to phone for up-to-date information. In this case it was Dee's friend Jean, who had left Brighton to work for social services in Lewisham, not far from Reeve Green where Nell lived. Jean was in Nalgo, and when it came to Clause 14, she had her finger right on the pulse. I knew next to nothing about politics, but I did know that my new family was a real family, and I was furious that anyone in the rest of Britain might not recognise that.

I also wanted Lotte and Dee to know that I was with them, one of them, and had been since I first loved Jennifer Bradley in junior school. I hadn't really come out to anyone yet – I was barely out to myself – and I wasn't ready to go out and about on demos. But I did want to show Lotte and Dee how much they meant to me. I decided to tell them my full story.

I was a keen cyclist and had bought a good mountain bike from the wages that Stuart had paid me before I left Coombebury. I cycled down to the village and bought a bottle of good red wine and some After Eights. Then, back home, I made a cashew-nut paella, Lotte's favourite, ready when Dee and Lotte came in from work.

Over dinner, we chatted a while about the week, and then Dee mentioned something about Jean in Lewisham and the dreaded Clause. That was my cue.

'I've something to tell you,' I said nervously. 'It's this Clause 14 thing that made me decide to say something, because you're my family now. Is this a good time to talk?'

'Yes, of course. Nice meal, lovely warm fire, couldn't be better.'

'Well, I don't know where to begin really. Uhm. I . . . I've always wanted to live like you two, find someone, someone like me, uhm . . .' I was thinking go on Gail, spit it out, 'Another *girl* my age. You don't even know the full story, and I can't hold back any longer, because this Clause 14 is about all of us. It's not as if, well, there's only you two, you know, the way you are, and me – somebody strange, a lodger or something, living here – somebody called Gail, who doesn't know who she is and what she wants. Well, I do know what I am, I've known a long time, and that's why I wanted to live with both of you. I just wanted you to know.'

Eloquent it wasn't, but I knew they'd understood.

'That's wonderful,' said Lotte, simply.

Dee was nodding and smiling fit to bust. 'Yes, yes it is,' she said, and had to blow her nose. They both came over and gave me a long hug. But I knew I had more to tell them.

I waited for them to settle down again. I looked around the tiny room, which we had all worked on one weekend, scrubbing the wooden floor and the old skirting boards, all of which still needed to be replaced, painting over the crumbling plaster of the walls and ceilings until we could attend to them properly. There were bright red curtains at the rotten windows, and when it rained we draped them over chairs and put buckets down to catch the drips. It was a small room, at the back of the second cottage, behind my bedroom, which looked over the front garden. Eventually, this would be our television den when we had done the large kitchen diner. But until then we always ate in here, at the table and with a real fire burning. I could see the flames reflected in the wine glasses and the pink splodges on Lotte's cheeks where the warmth and wine had caught up with her.

'I did tell Uncle Stuart some of this, not all of it, but I made him promise not to tell you. I wanted to tell you myself when I was ready. I thought it'd take me much longer to get to this point, but the Clause made it seem real in a way.

'It was difficult growing up knowing I wasn't wanted. I said to Uncle Stuart, "I know I'm in the wrong. My mother wanted a boy and she wanted to keep my father's love as well. But he left her because she got pregnant with me. She told me about that. She conceived me too soon, she wasn't ready for a baby. She made it seem like it was all my fault."

'Anyway, Mum said she wanted a boy so that she could prove that being gay doesn't run in the family. She doesn't like it that Uncle Stuart is gay. She hates gay lives, she says. But she needed his help, babysitting at weekends. She needs his money as well. He always liked me. He was kind to me from the start.

'Then she met a boyfriend called Jimmy. I was ten years old.

42

He tried to touch me, down there, and I knifed him. Mum thought they would blame her – for not bringing me up right. She gave me a real pasting for that. She really frightened me. She told me that they would take me away, lock me up and throw away the key. So then I wouldn't go out of the house. That's when I became too scared to go to school.'

I stopped speaking for a while. Dee was sipping her wine slowly, looking straight at me, and Lotte was crying silently. I felt myself getting tearful too, but I didn't want to stop now that I had begun, so I took a deep breath and waded on.

'When I told this to Uncle Stuart a little while ago, he said that I was the least violent person he'd ever met and that I was not responsible for what Caroline, my mother, had done to me, or let others do to me.

'Anyway, there's more. There's much more. About two years ago when I was fifteen I met a young man who was gay, called Terence, a friend of Uncle Stuart's. He was very kind to me and we started going places together. I thought I was very lucky. He hadn't got any sisters and I had always hoped for a sister or brother, so he became the brother I never had. I felt safe with him.

'I could really talk to Terry. I told him all about Jennifer Bradley, how I'd liked her, and how I wanted to live the way you two live. But when my mother found out about my new friend she was horrified. She realised he was gay and had a real go at Uncle Stuart about it. Wasn't it enough that he, Stuart, was a gay man, without him encouraging me to spend time with them? Why couldn't I find a nice boyfriend? But Terence was the first friend I'd had for years. I didn't have friends of my own, because I'd had home tutors all the time.

'Anyway, my mother tried to put a stop to me seeing Terry. She said he was playing about, trying the field, probably bisexual or something. But he wasn't. He was as gay as gay can be. He was as camp as a row of tents and he made me laugh.

'Then it all began to go really wrong. My mother got a new boyfriend. John, his name was ... I couldn't stand him. He hates gays for a start. But I knew Mum was lonely. She doesn't like to be without a partner. She took ages to find this man, and I think she loved him. I didn't think he was worth keeping but she seemed to think he was. She hated me when he looked at me as if he fancied me. He was a slimy sort, suggestive, and it made me feel uncomfortable. He'd sidle up to me, too near. He didn't like me going over to my Uncle's house or going to clubs with Terry. Why couldn't I find a real man, he'd say, things like that.

'But Mum seemed to need him. She wanted the warmth, I suppose. Someone her age to talk to. Someone to go out and about with. And the sex of course. She blocked out what was happening to me. Didn't want to look at it. I think she is afraid of being lonely when she gets older.

'Then he moved in. Got his feet under the table. More suggestions to me. Nothing you could pin down, just a bit sleazy, you know?

'He'd been there five or six weeks and one night I got back to find that Mum had gone to bed and John was still downstairs, drinking. I had my own key, and Terry saw me to the door. I went in the kitchen to make a hot drink. Next thing, I realised he was right up behind me, feeling me up.'

'Oh, Jesus,' said Lotte.

'Go on, Gail,' said Dee, very gently. 'What happened next?'

'I tried to push him away – he was badmouthing a lot – said I was a slag who went for queers. What I needed was a real man to show me what was what . . . he got his arm round my face from behind and I bit him with all my might. I tried to fight back. All hell let loose. He slapped me hard and I slipped and fell. Caroline, Mum, woke up and came downstairs to find him with a belt in his hand, about to hit me again. I thought she'd stop him, protect me, but then she took his side and said I had encouraged him . . .'

'What, with you in a heap on the floor?'

'Yes, but to Mum I am simply wrong. I've always been wrong.'

'And then?'

'John was shouting that I had come on strong and deserved to be put in my place. He was going to teach me a lesson. Teach me who was boss. He said he only slapped me to shut me up and that the fall was an accident.

'Mum said that I deserved a bit of a slap, 'bout time I came to my senses. Then she started accusing me of setting out to spoil the first real thing that had happened to her in years. They left me there on the floor and I think I passed out. When I came to I got a taxi to Uncle Stuart's and told him I was running away. But I didn't tell him all this. I couldn't.'

The dinner was over, and so was the full story. I felt free of a burden, as if I had set down a heavy basket that had been on my shoulders since I was a small child. Lotte and Dee stood, pushing their chairs away from the table, and came to me. I was sobbing quietly. They held me close, and Dee said softly, 'You're part of this family, Gail, and no one is going to hurt you now.'

Esther
January, 1988

In the front garden, alongside the path to the front door of
Phoebe's mum's house, there were some strange plants. I didn't
like them much, with their long unsightly frostbitten stems. But
Phoebe's mum loved them. They were called ice plants, and she
grew them for the butterflies.

There were times that Christmas when I felt as cold inside as
the ice plants, despite my love for Phoebe. I missed San Francisco
and all our friends there. I missed the women in the spirituality
group, with whom I'd been celebrating the cycle of the year, and
I missed my drumming group.

But most of all, I was disappointed not to be with Lotte and
Deanne for the midwinter season, and it seemed an isolating
experience, being so near yet so far away from my family
connections. I understood that their new young friend, Gail,
whom they had taken in and were caring for, had had some sort
of violent family crisis, though I didn't know the details. I almost
felt as if Lotte was protecting Gail from me, which hurt me very
much indeed. Presumably, Lotte was afraid that I would go
ranting on about politics and violence against women, without
being sensitive to Gail. It's hard to face the fact that your sister
whom you love doesn't trust you with her nearest and dearest,
even more so when you know that you've mellowed down, and
are more careful and considerate. But I suppose there was also the
question of Deanne and Isobel.

Thankfully, the coolness of Lotte's response was in complete
contrast to the warmth, welcome and spontaneity of Laura, who
invited us to join her family in Bristol for the New Year.

Laura was now Mrs Joseph Phillips. I make a point of that because she always did. On her letters to me in SF the sender would be Mrs blah blah, and this despite Laura's feminism. It didn't fit, and when things don't fit it makes for an interesting personality – you can't take anything for granted. Laura always had her own money, her independent work, her own friends, but her devotion to Joseph was profound, and they were like two pieces of music that fitted together. Selfishly, and with a strong sense of contradiction of myself and my own politics, I hoped they would never part, because I couldn't imagine the loss I would feel, let alone the trauma they would have to go through. But I was also relaxed about it – nothing seemed less likely and they went on from year to year, working hard on their relationship and raising their two daughters.

Their house was still decorated with streamers and greeting cards from Christmas, with more than a sprinkling from the Caribbean. There was a noticeable absence of cards for the winter solstice. Although they had no special interest in my spirituality – for I'm no longer a Christmas person – what did interest them was the fact that it was their reading list, back in the seventies, that had set me off searching for long lost goddesses from everywhere other than Europe. It had been a long journey from the far-off days of my book-learning while living near to Nell, to my new-found connections with the We'Moon women of the west coast of the States.

Laura made up the sofa bed for me and Phoebe in their attic study, and we lacked for nothing by way of food, drink and company. Melody and Sophie were coming and going with their friends, and at times the house resembled Clapham Junction. It almost put me in mind of the traffic through Nell's council house in Reeve Green, but there the resemblance finished.

Both Laura and Joseph had always worked full time since leaving college. Joseph now taught at the university, in politics and history, and Laura managed a drop-in centre for unemployed young people in the St Paul's area.

With two professional salaries and their involvement in the theory and practice of what they were doing, they were becoming part of the middle-class professional black strata in the vibrant city where they had made their home.

'We love it here, you know,' said Laura. 'It's not your San Francisco but it's our city and we feel a part of it.'

Phoebe said, 'Yes. Esther and I are talking seriously at the moment of where *our* place might be, and whether there is one.'

'Not Africa again?'

'Not immediately. Sometime in the future, perhaps. I feel I need a complete change of culture at the present time.'

'Understandably so,' replied Laura, delicately letting the end of her sentence remain silent, that break-ups are always devastating.

'I wonder how your mother will find this city, Joseph?' Phoebe continued. 'It'll be something of a culture shock, surely? You mentioned you were bringing her over here. Will she stay here with you?'

'No, with my brother and his wife. They're the reason we chose Bristol originally. Rawle and I were always very close. Only eleven months between us. When my father died last year, we persuaded our mother to come and join us. Not a permanent arrangement. She would grieve too much for Trinidad. So, she'll return there, at some stage, to live with our younger sister. But she's very active, says she will give it a try, here. Months, not just weeks. She's curious about this country. And she'll be able to see her grandchildren at firsthand, not just videos and letters.'

'Will you go and fetch her?'

'Yes. We're taking the girls for the summer holidays, but Laura has to come home for work – '

'I only get four weeks a year, even now.'

'So the girls and I will stay on and help my mother pack. Then we'll fly back with her.'

Laura said, 'It's a good opportunity for the girls to visit Trinidad again. They're really the right age to appreciate it now, get the most out of it.'

'I've never been,' Phoebe replied. 'But I would love to visit the Caribbean. So many of my friends have family there. I should think the very idea of all that sunshine is keeping you going, isn't it?'

'I should say so. It's getting us through the cold greyness, isn't it, Joe?'

'It is. Blue skies, turquoise ocean, white sand...'
'Don't. Just don't. Okay?'

After dinner on New Year's Eve, Melody went off to someone's New Year party. The rest of us were in the mood for music, something we had often shared on my visits to Bristol. Sophie and two young friends took up their wind instruments, I was on the drums, Joseph on guitar, rattles and shakers for Phoebe and Laura, and we were off jamming until the small hours, interrupting the session only to link arms for 'Auld Lang Syne' at midnight. Melody returned about twelve thirty, ravenous for hot soup and garlic bread, then we carried on until we were exhausted but fully relaxed (which may also have been down to the bottle of Baileys, the full-bodied Jamaican rum, and the box of red wine that we had demolished between us!).

I woke in the late morning of New Year's Day, thinking that I was very lucky indeed. Between Laura's long-term friendship and hospitality and my new-found warmth and sexual intimacy with Phoebe, I almost had a sense of family again.

I know that this is what Laura would have wanted me to feel. I'd been closer to her at times in my teens, and since then, than I had been to Lotte. Being with her and her family in that lively musical household had helped to take the edge off my fear of rejection from Lotte and Dee and their exclusive triangle at Mere Cottage. But I didn't want to be separated falsely from my own sister again, as had happened when she met and married James. Again I wondered where home was now, for me, Esther Clegg. Was it really back here in Britain, with these wonderful friends? Could I move with Phoebe to Bristol and could we both find work and make a meaningful life here? I didn't know. And in any case there was a new shadow over the whole proceedings – for we were lesbians and the whole question of what family meant for us, and therefore, where home was, was being raised at a national level.

We returned to a chilly London, where, with relentless progress, Clause 14 rapidly became Clause 27, then Clause 28. The attack on lesbians and their families was all over the pink press. I contacted my lesbian friends in the city and talked late into the night with them about their lives and the implications if the Clause wasn't stopped.

I thought back to all that Deanne's Dora had suffered because she wasn't able to be out; and to what Deanne had gone through, seeing her lover face the terror of hospitals, locked rooms and strangers in authority, without the comfort of being recognised as Dora's next of kin. Dora had lost her mind after the birth of her baby, Isobel, and had been in a mental hospital for years and years, plugged in to the national grid: shocked and shocked and shocked until the room had spun around her and all her colours had blurred into the nothingness of death. Isobel had been only fourteen when she lost her mother. She had attended the funeral with Dee, her surrogate mother.

Now it was me whose behaviour was hurting Deanne because I was lovers with Phoebe – Isobel's ex-lover. It was a mess, but it didn't mean that any of us were pretending to love, or that we were not women with good hearts and a real need for family life.

I watched the ice plants as the debates over the Clause wore on. Those plants were struggling, like me, in a cold city. They were longing, like me, for some spring sunshine, only the warmth I craved was political. How would it be to live in a culture that was not only accepting of lesbians, but openly welcoming? What might it be like to be able to talk of lesbian families without the gutter press taking a suspicious or sleazy angle on it? What if growing up lesbian was considered so normal that mothers welcomed it in their offspring? Dream on, Esther Clegg, dream on.

One fine morning in the new year I tended the ice plants, gently taking off the dead stems with a pair of secateurs. I handled them carefully, the plants I had been refusing to love. Suddenly, I saw that they had begun to grow again, brave pale green leaves, new shoots, round rosettes, preparing. They put me in mind of a chant I had heard at a planning meeting for the demo against Clause 28. I had invited Lotte and Dee to come up and meet us, so that we could go with Phoebe's friends and one or two of mine, in a big group to support the Stop The Clause organisation. It was a heartwarming chant especially designed for those of us who, whatever the difficulties of being out, were staying out, never to return to a life in the closet. We had chanted the phrase quietly, memorising it: *For love and for life we are not going back. For love and for life we are not going back.*

I knelt by the tiny grey-green plants, the ones I had steadfastly rejected as ugly. Tenderly, I clipped and tidied them, the hard coldness of the front path making my knees ache. 'What kind of life force do you carry?' I asked them, silently. 'A force so strong that you chance new green rosettes in a freezing London winter?' It must be the same life force that makes fragile blades of grass grow up through concrete. The ice plants gave me courage and strength, growing there close to the cold ground, so resolutely, despite the chilly winter weather.

Later, back indoors, over hot soup and toasted cheese, I relayed to Phoebe all that I had been thinking.

She said, 'I hope Lotte and Deanne do come up for the demo. I want to see them, to reconnect with them again. I used to get wonderful letters from Deanne. But I can understand her anger and distress, because she only has Isobel's story to go on.'

'Isobel didn't want you to break up.'

'I know that, but she wanted a change in how we were doing things, just as much as I did. She was desperate to escape from our old patterns. We both were. Besides, Deanne is no fool. She knows that Isobel and I had been giving one another a hard time in the past few months. In her heart she knows you aren't responsible for our break-up, Ess. Break-ups don't happen if everything in the garden's a bed of roses. She knows I'm not fickle, and she knows you're not a ruthless woman. You would never crash in on a couple, not if they were still together. I'm sure Deanne recognises that, because she knows you, she knows you have integrity about things like that.'

'I hope so. I so much want to see Lotte and Dee together. Not just Lotte on her own. They are lovely women, both of them. Good women with warm hearts.'

'Then let's try to trust them. Hopefully they will come up for the demo. Come here, Ess. Don't be so anguished about it all. I want to hold you.'

We went to bed early that night, with our favourite music playing and the light of candles flickering around our room.

There is no hurry. I have always believed that sex is an art form, like music or painting, and that our bodies were given to us to be cherished, to be played like finely tuned instruments.

She is lying on her side, turned away from me. She has the most beautiful back, soft and smooth like the polished wood of a cello. She has sensitive shoulders – erogenous, focused, and ready. In my mind are melodies and harmonies as I stroke her gently but firmly with my fingertips.

She shivers as I slide my fingertips across her shoulders, then down the length of her spine. She ripples with the sensuous pleasure of touch. She is making small sounds; the tentative first notes of a well-loved symphony.

I take my time. There is no hurry.

I hear her low gentle moaning deepen as my fingers caress the curve of her hip and play across her pubic hair. My hand reaches into her and she sighs, joyfully, as I find her clit. She is so moist, so open to this touch.

She is the cello, in my arms, and I play her delicately with the knowledge that comes from our same-only-different reflection. She creates from inside her body, with her own beautiful rhythms, one of her very low rolling orgasms, which resonates and trembles, rises and returns.

We have all night, if we want to. I am searching her now for every note of orgasm that can be found, discovering the murmuring places where she has yet some more, just a little more, until finally we are satiated. The harmonies are resolved. Our bodies are flung in relaxed abandon. She is complete.

I lay there afterwards, deeply in love with Phoebe. Glad to be out and proud. I was thinking that if someone searched in my bone marrow they'd see the word lesbian written right through it like seaside rock. Just as I was about to fall asleep, my body replete with our lovemaking, I realised that I was almost looking forward to the whole challenge of the demo, while the chant repeated itself in my mind: '*For love and for life I am not going back.*'

Deanne
January, 1988

It was a couple of weeks after Christmas, and Gail had settled in well. We'd been with her to the ENT specialist in Harley Street twice, our trips funded by Stuart. He had mortgaged his house and rewritten his will in Gail's favour. I'd been shocked and very touched to find out that until then, I'd been the beneficiary of his estate. He had never before told me that, but it confirmed my own feelings that he and I were family for one another.

I didn't need Stuart's money, but Gail did. We delved deeper into the complex process of how much Gail's hearing could be saved in her left ear. She'd impressed upon us that she was unwilling to seek revenge or retribution against her attacker. She hadn't told the doctors in casualty exactly how she came to fall against a worktop. She had simply said that she slipped and that it was an accident. To us she said, 'I don't want insurance claims or anything else. It'd connect me back to him. That's why I won't go to the police. I don't want any of that. This is a new life for me now. I want a clean slate. I want to draw a line under it.'

Meanwhile, I was struggling with my decision about meeting Phoebe. I had always liked her, and I didn't want to lose contact with her, but Izzie was writing sad and angry letters from Zimbabwe, where she was working on an irrigation project.

What could I say to Phoebe? How would I convey to her that I wanted to be friends – understood there were two different versions that would never add up, didn't want to be judgemental – but was on overload because she had gone so soon into another relationship, and she'd chosen, of all people, Lotte's sister, Esther?

I knew that Esther wasn't to blame for Izzie's painful break-up. Of course, I did. I knew that Phoebe would not need to take comfort somewhere else if all was sweetness and ease with Izzie. But I had hoped that Phoebe would give them both more time. Instead, she had jumped right off a cliff and floated down unexpectedly into Esther's waiting arms.

We were tired during the Christmas break that year. The physical labour on the house took all our spare time, and learning to be with Gail, when we'd been on our own for years, was an enormous adjustment for Lotte and me. I wrote very often to Izzie. Supporting Izzie was an ongoing process, a word I'd picked up from some counsellors who came for an annual conference to the Cavendish Hotel. They were pleasant enough, but it was all process this and process that until I couldn't look at a tin of processed peas in the supermarket without smirking. I could see the whole tin crammed full of little green counsellors. Isn't language a wonderful thing?

Counsellors apart, I could probably have coped with Phoebe on her own. But Phoebe *with* Esther, well that was another matter altogether. They were keen for us to come to the demonstration against the Clause, which was to be held in Kennington Park behind the Imperial War Museum. I wanted to stay at home with Gail, but didn't want to abandon Lotte. After all the support she had given me over the house, it didn't feel right to be unsupportive where her sister was concerned, especially as Esther had had a very traumatic end to her work at Reeve Green; she had left for San Francisco with a cloud behind her. So, by now, there were a lot of competing and conflicting needs in everyone's lives, all brought together in a tangle around the demo.

The first thing to do, I decided, was to find out if my intuition was right as to what Gail wanted for that weekend. We were delighted that she had chosen us as her new family, and that she wanted to live like us, as a lesbian. However, I wondered if it would all be too rushed for Gail – recognising who she was was one thing, but perhaps being out and going on demos would be another matter.

In my life, I have met so many different kinds of lesbians, gay women, and gay men. I thought back to the small crowd of us who used to meet in Coombebury in the fifties. Irma and Frank ran The Feathers pub. Gay men would meet there and we women had a corner, though it was hard to keep our own space. The gay 'boys', as they were known, were not much good at welcoming us, and some of them were downright hostile. I've been a gay girl and now a lesbian older woman for years and years and I know the history well. So I've no illusions about it all being hunkydory 'brothers and sisters'. Not at all.

I'm very fond of my friend Stuart, and I've known various lovers of his across the years. But not everyone's like him. Some gay guys really don't like women at all and there are those who treat women with the same sort of oppressive disdain as straight men. I could quite imagine that nowadays, some radical lesbians, like Esther, might not be into working with the gay men at all. Far from it. But the dreaded Clause was bringing together all kinds of lesbians and gay men, some of whom had never really been involved in political groups. I hadn't. I wasn't at all political before I fell for Lotte. It was only through her reading and her sometimes wanting to be with other lesbians – who were, as she put it, 'out and proud' – that we had decided to change jobs and move to Brighton. I had been ready for a change, and the Bronnester Hotel gave me a fabulous send-off and a wonderful reference.

All these thoughts were now surfacing because of Clause 28. I wondered to myself whether every gay woman and every self-defined lesbian in the country might have to go through a careful thinking process (that word again) as to what she wanted, how she might join in, or whether she would stay at home and read about it in the press.

Part of me just wanted to stay at home. It was cowardice really. I could sit it out, and eventually Phoebe and Esther might not be in London any longer, and I could write gentle letters to them, that didn't trouble me.

But in my mind there was also my first lover, Dora, whose funeral I had attended with Izzie when she was only fourteen. I'm pretty certain that the hospital had found out that Dora had been in a lesbian relationship. I became sure as time went on that part of the reason for the electric shock therapy was to straighten her out again. She died of terror – of their locked doors and clamps and tubes. She died drugged to the eyeballs. She could no longer read because the drugs made the words swim. She loved bright colours and at her funeral we filled the place with huge blocks of colour to celebrate Dora and her love of life. I had watched her die slowly for fourteen years. They had frightened her to death in that place. Not that I would have ever been able to prove it. But later the psychologists created a form of treatment for gay people called 'aversion therapy'. I am sure that my Dora was a guinea pig for that.

So now, with the biggest attack of the postwar period on lesbian and gay men, was I going to forget what they did to Dora and make no shout about it? Could I really turn my back on the whole campaign, and utter not one word of defiance? I thought, 'No. No, I won't be quiet about this, Dora. For your sake I have to go to that awful cold park and stand there, simply stand there. Myself, Deanne Derby, who ran away with another girl when we were only just in our teens rather than be separated from her. I must be there. I have to be there.'

Lotte
January, 1988

Gail was upstairs, working on the skirting boards, when Dee asked her about the trip to London. The chisel slipped, snagging Gail's hand. She let out a howl, and they dashed downstairs so that she could run off the blood under the cold tap.

Gail said, 'Do you remember when we first moved here, and I was afraid to go out anywhere? Well, that's changing, but I'm not ready to go further afield, not yet. Do you mind very much if I don't come?'

It turned out that she had no fear of being left at Mere Cottage on her own, not even at night. That showed us how far she had come, how much she had already changed since her arrival, when we wouldn't have dreamt of leaving her, even though she was well above the age when you could normally leave someone on their own. But age wasn't the issue for Gail, was it? It was safety, and we both understood that. Dee and I were glad she felt so safe at Mere Cottage that we could leave her alone for the weekend.

We decided to stay with our friend, Jean. Esther longed for us to come and stay at Phoebe's mum's house, but it was all a bit too much for us. However, we decided that we would both meet up with Essie and Phoebe on the day.

I remember it as the bleakest event I have ever gone to. The day was dark grey, no sunshine. Not one of those blue winter days when you're glad to be out and about. We walked to the park with the others and stood there as speakers talked through a microphone to us one after another. The details of the Clause, its history, its effects if it were passed, were all described. Then I turned and saw that down the side streets were dozens of ranks of tall dark brown and black horses. I had never seen anything like it before. On each horse there was a police rider in full riot gear. They wore helmets, and in front of them they held their riot shields as if facing some alien attack.

Standing beside me was Esther. I reached for her hand and squeezed it tightly, pointing to them. She nodded, sombrely. I felt physically sick at the thought of them charging us. I'd seen the photographs of the miners' strike, the bloody faces and beaten bodies. I remembered everything Esther had told me about the Suffragettes, so I leaned towards Dee and whispered, 'When you see those riot police, it makes you realise how brave the Suffragettes were, standing up and facing all the hatred, doesn't it?'

She nodded, smiling warmly at me to reassure me, but her words revealed her true feelings. She said, 'They are so intimidating, Lotte. I hate it here. It's so cold and I'm absolutely petrified.'

The mood in the crowd was changing. We could detect ripples of apprehension as awareness of the police presence grew. People faced the fact that we were being surrounded. Our eyes were now scanning the exits. Other people were doing the same.

Someone came on to the raised scaffolding dais with a hailer. We were told to stay calm and link arms and leave the park in fives and tens. We must not run. We must not make a dash for it.

Esther was fuming. 'How dare they? How can they treat us like this? How can they be so threatened by a bunch of dykes and gay men? It is ridiculous.'

'That's as may be, love,' said Phoebe, 'You're not wrong Ess, but let's just get out of here in one piece, shall we?'

We linked arms and became part of the slow surge for the gates. I'll never forget the sense of relief when we finally got through the gates and made our way back to the tube. The sky was leaden, as if the Clause itself were a great grey shadow, glowering over us as we headed home.

Tracey
February, 1988

I'd had no idea Mum was staking me out. I'd have been furious.
But I wish I'd listened.

'I'm saving up for a car, like yours,' said Maxie. 'I don't want to
spend this money and I don't want the social on me back for
having savings, do I? So, will you look after this for me?' She
handed me a roll of notes. I didn't count it but there was a lot. I
knew where it came from but I told myself I didn't know. She
wasn't into hard stuff. It was puff, that's all. That's what I told
myself. It's not as dangerous as drink and they should legalise it.

I knew Maxie could always get plenty. She was generous with
it. But I didn't think ahead at all. All I knew was that I wasn't
lonely any more. Sex was really wonderful. It was easy.

Sometimes, late at night, people would call. I knew Maxie was
dealing. They'd come in, stay a minute. Leave. She'd give me
another roll of money to look after. I'd put it in the top drawer
under my knickers. I was often at home when people called. I
didn't think it could go wrong.

Then one day she said she'd be out, but someone might come
to collect a package.

'Can't they come back later, when you're here?'

'No, it's urgent. Don't worry. It's only puff. Don't fret. All
right?'

'Not really. I don't like it when you're not here. It's different if
you're not here.'

'Well it's just this once, Tracey. Look, sweetheart, it's just for me,
okay? Simple, easy, okay? I'll be back by ten.'

I didn't ask where she was going. She had people to meet. I

knew that. So I didn't ask. I was there when they raided. It was clever, I'll say that. Plain clothes. Undercover job. They'd been watching us for weeks.

Fortunately for me, it *was* only puff. I was right about that. If Maxie had been doing E or smack, I'd have gone down for much, much longer.

They did us for possession with intent to supply. There were none of her fingerprints on the roll of money. Only mine. They asked me to explain that. I said I couldn't. They said I was lying.

Maxie was so clever. There was a block of it, cut and wrapped, ready to sell, under the jumpers in my chest of drawers. Three of her friends swore an affidavit that *I* had supplied them, me personally, from my flat. They gave dates and times. I was there on each occasion. She would have paid six hundred for that block. It had a street value of over a thousand.

March, 1988

I can't feel the sun in here. One day, when they let me out, I'll pick up my guitar and I'll sing it all out of me.

I can't hear the rain in here. I can't hear nothing 'cept metal and stone and doors clanging. Banged up is what they say. Now I know why.

If Maxie hadn't had the rest of the stuff we'd've probably got off. I could spend all day every day asking, What if?

I don't like being indoors. Haven't liked it since I left me mum's place, Reeve Green. I left home when I came out. She more or less threw me out. Now this. She hates drugs. She's not likely to believe me. Nor did the judge. I said they weren't mine. It was true.

But it was my flat and there was all Maxie's money rolled up in my knickers drawer. And the stuff in Maxie's room. It wasn't just in one chunk: it was cut into strips, all twenty odd of 'em separately wrapped. It wasn't me into all that stuff – Maxie said I was, but I wasn't. But I knew it was going on – I just didn't think it involved me. What a dickhead. Class C, they said. Possession with intent. That means with intent to supply. That's the difference. That makes you not just another kid that's smoking. It makes you a dealer. And I'm not. I'm not. Truly, I'm not.

You should see the state Maxie's in. She did her wrists. Prison hospital.

To survive in here you've got to be cold as ice. So nothing can get to you. Nothing can hurt you. Closed. You've got to be closed. I've got to learn to shut up and shut down. Got to learn it fast, too.

I'm too tuned in to 'the voices' at the moment. If I wasn't tuned in it'd be easier; if I couldn't hear the screaming of the women who were thrown in here years ago. Tubes and clamps and hot liquid being poured into their lungs. At night it's like they come to me, long lines of them, faces, voices.

I'm doing time for nothing. Well not for nothing. I mean they did find the stuff even if it wasn't mine. You can't prove it if it's in your flat, can you? And I worked hard for that flat, 'n' all.

There's this woman writing to me. She was in here after Greenham. She said you can stay sane, just keep going, till they let you out. She's okay. I like her letters.

There's all sorts in here. There's women in here for poverty. Couldn't pay their TV licences. Can you believe that? I can, now. There's women from Nigeria who got caught with packets of drugs sewn under their skin. Mules, they're called. Mules carry burdens for other people. They were promised money and education in this country if they just did this one small packet. Now they're carrying another burden. Long sentences, some of them. Poor sods. That's poverty for you.

This place is my education. I'll never be the same now I've been in here. Seen it for myself. What a way to get an education.

There's a woman that fancies me. A white woman called Sylve. Butch? You haven't seen butch till you've seen Sylve. Tattoos. Blimey. I thought she was a man – well, not really, but she's the nearest I've seen to a man that's a real bull dyke – and I've seen a few since I came out. I've loved and lost and I owe no one nothing.

I've got to get through this.

Somehow, I am going to make this place work for me or I'll go mad. I mean I worked down the market because I don't like to be shut in. That's how much I like walls. Or doors. Coming out, for me, was about being out and staying out, and that means outside.

Outside everything. Outside me mum's heart, outside me mum's house. I worked for everything I got, and I'm proud of it. But I didn't look over me shoulder and I learned too late.

That woman from Greenham, she had a bird used to come to her. A spirit bird, she called it. Came right into her cell. It was a kestrel. I've never seen a kestrel. When I get out of here I'm going to the hills, the high places where kestrels and such fly free.

I never did like things in cages.

I did a bit of thinking last night. I was lying here, listening to a woman crying. I don't know who it was. There's somebody shouts all night, too. Don't know who. I made up me mind that if Sylve wants to look after me in here, I'll let her. She can have me if she wants me. I'll fake it if I have to. There's no body'll harm me, if I'm Sylve's woman.

Take care of yourself, my gran told me mum, when she was dying and me mum was my age. Take care of yourself 'cos no one else's going to.

Not true. Not in here. In this place if you're going to take care of yourself you might start with Sylve. Take what's on offer and don't look back. That's my motto now.

I shall write to that woman from Greenham. Her and her spirit kestrel. Rebecca. I liked her. Her letter was kind.

Esther
March, 1988

I don't feel I belong here in this country.

I've seen Lotte a few times, sometimes with Deanne, sometimes not. I've met Gail who is very shy but seems friendly enough. But I don't feel as if I'm on the inside of the family. Something has changed there. It used to be me, Lotte and Deanne, but now a new triangle has been formed. Lotte is hiding something, or maybe she is just protective of Gail, but in any case her reticence seems strange. We were so close. Now we're not. There is some mystery around Gail, and I can't put my finger on it. But it's more than that. For some reason the walls are up and I'm sure it's not just about me being lovers with Phoebe, difficult though that is for us all.

It feels as if they haven't got the time for me now, to discover how much I have changed. I'm softer, and the old raw anger has metamorphosed into a more mellow, calmer centre inside me. In the old days, my political friends in London might have challenged such a statement and told me I was 'losing my politics', but it's not like that at all. It's about how I present it. I used to rant a lot and everything seemed so direct and obvious to me. My anger is quite different now, but I like it, because it's clean and protective and helps me find out how I really feel about things. I just wish Lotte would let me reveal who I am now, instead of closing herself off. But also, she lives with Dee, and I understand how difficult it is for her to be piggy in the middle.

'There's nothing left here,' I said to Nell one morning over coffee and cake in her front room.

'Well you went away didn't you, Ess? It's like a spoonful out of a soup bowl, innit? You takes out your spoon and the hole fills up. You can't see where the spoon's been, you know? I think you did the right thing leaving after the accident. Things wasn't the same after that, was they?'

'I couldn't go on here, Nell.'

Sometimes you don't need extra words to tell the story if it sits there between you in all its graphic detail. In the kind and gentle silence that opened up between us, we both relived that dreadful time when a child was killed on the road outside Reeve Juniors. Josie Brown had been only eight years old. The woman driver, probably harassed about being late, simply didn't see the lollipop lady and drove straight into Josie. I was on duty and watched the whole scene as if it were happening in slow motion. I can still see every hair on the young child's head as she lay bleeding and broken in my arms. She died on the way to the hospital.

Nell looked at me with deep empathy. We both witnessed the tears in one another's eyes. She was the first to break the silence. 'You gave your all to that place, Ess. There was nothing you could do. As far as I was concerned they should've locked that woman up and thrown away the key. Got off far too light. You was right to leave, make a new life. Besides you saw the children through to the end of term, poor little sods. And they was going up to Mrs Purvis anyway! You was wonderful, Ess, you did everything you could.'

'Thank you.'

When the exchange scheme had suggested the general possibility of North America, I hesitated at first. It had seemed like running away. Such a long, long way. But I was all burned out. Then along came the particular proposal – a play project exchange in SF – and suddenly I had found myself in another city, surrounded by gay and lesbian culture, and it was wonderful. Like a reprieve.

'You'd still be there if you hadn't met Phoebe, wouldn't you, Ess?'

'I don't know. I was on a finite contract, though there is plenty more work out there for me if I want it.'

'And you do, don't you?'

'Yes, and Phoebe wants to go back with me. She got lecturing work before so that's not a problem. It's easy with her, Nell. I'm happy with this woman. I was on my own for a long time after Christine. And now I'm really happy. We could both go back, Nell. We could go back there to live.'

'For ever, Ess? You leaving us for ever?'

'I'll come back and see you, Nell. And when I've got money, I'll send you the fare. You can come and stay. I'll show you the Golden Gate Bridge. And Alcatraz,' I said, deliberately. 'You always said you wanted to see Alcatraz.'

'That was before my Trace was banged up in Holloway. I don't think I'll be doing prisons.'

'Have you been to see her, yet?'

'No. I can't abide drugs. I told you. She was with a bad lot. I could kill that Maxie.'

'Tracey'd like to see you. You're her mum.'

'You make your life, Ess, and I'll make mine. I've been your friend for years, but my Trace is my Trace and I won't be told. Not where drugs is concerned.'

'She says they weren't hers.'

'Pull the other one, will you?'

'I believe her.'

'All right then. You stay here and I'll go to San Francisco. I like the sunshine. You live here and visit my Trace each week and I'll work on your next play project. All right?'

'I'm sorry. I'm sorry. Let's not fall out Nell, please.'

'I'm sorry, too.' Nell paused. Then she said sadly, 'So you're going then, with Phoebe?'

'Yes. There's ways and means to do it.'

'There's only one way to get residency in the States for an English woman.' Nell pointed to the gold band on the third finger of her left hand.

I nodded.

'Gay friends of Phoebe's, are they?'

'No. They're Matt's friends – Matt is Phoebe's brother. We have to pay them. They'll do it for the money. I'll need you to write to me using my "married" name on the envelope. I have to keep up appearances for a couple of years.'

'Things is tightening up over there, so I heard. You'll have to live with them. You and Phoebe and him and his boyfriend, whoever he is.'

I nodded.

She raised her eyebrows and rolled her eyes, and I smiled like the Mona Lisa, inscrutable.

'I need a new country – a new life with new hope. I did wonder when we came back to London this winter if we could start again here, but it's hopeless. It's not just the thing with Deanne and Lotte, it's more than that. This Clause 28 thing is appalling. Everywhere here is grey, the skies, the streets. I just can't get any sense of a future here. In California, I feel so hopeful.'

Nell snorted. 'Quake City they call it on the telly. Living on a fault line. Give me London any day. Besides they're all dying over there.'

'Oh, Nell!'

'It's true. My Cyril that I clean for, he's gay, and he's lost a couple of friends already, in *London*. But not like over there. He says they're going down like skittles. He does. What you lookin' at me like that for?'

'Because you say what everyone else is thinking. I say I'm going back to San Francisco and they think Aids. It's written all over their faces.'

'That's 'cos it's true. I just mean that ten years from now, if you live there, you'll have dealt with a lot of loss. That's what I mean. I don't hear any common sense coming from you, Esther Clegg. You *had* to leave Reeve Green because that child died in your arms. It changed your life. But now you're going to live happily ever after in death city. If your friends don't die of Aids the earth'll open up and get you. How can a woman choose to live in a place like that?'

'Quite easily, Nell. We aren't going to agree on this. I love the place, I've missed it more than I care to admit and I want to go back and make a life there, and marrying Matt's friend can make it happen.'

'You leave me speechless, Ess.'

'That took some doing,' I grinned. 'To get you to stop talking for just two minutes I have to do matrimonials!'

We both laughed but it was clear that Nell was really choked up. 'Oh come here, Ess,' she said, 'I got to hug you tight. This is my worst nightmare. One of my closest friends is going to live halfway round the other side of the world. When am I going to see you, if you're so far away?'

There was no answer to that. We just stood, arms round each other, holding as tight as if we were the axis mundi, around which our world was spinning much too fast.

Then I plucked up my courage, risking her divine wrath and my excommunication, and said, 'There is only one gift I need to take back with me.'

'You got my friendship, Ess. That's for ever!'

'I know. You've got mine too. Please, Nell, tell Tracey that you know she is telling the truth.'

Tracey
May, 1988

I had a letter last month from a stranger. Not the woman from Greenham, Rebecca – anyway, she doesn't feel like a stranger any more because she writes to me all the time.

This letter was from Gail, the one staying with Mum's friends. I'll tell you what she wrote.

Dear Tracey,

You don't know me, but I'm living with your mum's friends, Deanne and Lotte, in their house, Mere Cottage. They told me what happened to you and when I heard that no one believes your side of the story, not even your own mother, I knew I *had* to write because my own mother doesn't believe me either, so I know how it feels and how much it hurts.

What my mum doesn't believe is that I don't have any designs on her boyfriend. She thinks I'm nothing but trouble. When I was ten, one of her boyfriends tried to touch me up and I knifed him. But Mum just wouldn't listen. The boyfriend buggered off, saying that I was a nutter, and she sent me to live with my Uncle Stuart for a few weeks. I told him the truth and he did believe me, but I couldn't stay there for ever. I had to go home. Then, about ten months ago it happened again, only this time the boyfriend got violent and started hitting me. I don't really want to tell you all the details here – I'd rather tell you face to face.

I know my mum has always resented me - she wasn't ready to have a baby. Then, when she decided to go ahead with her pregnancy, she wanted a boy, a son. Mum told me in no uncertain terms that I was the reason Dad left her, and that it was my fault he disowned us both. I knew she was lying but it still hurt.

I can't understand why your mum doesn't believe you but I wanted you to know that Lotte, Dee and I do. They've been so good to me. I am being loved for the first time in my life (apart from Uncle Stuart), and I am coming alive. I am training as a carpenter, and working on the house here. I work very hard, long hours, so that I can repay Dee and Lotte for all their kindness.

They told me that you worked on Lewisham market come rain or shine and that you love to be outdoors. We have a wonderful garden here, which we are uncovering bit by bit. It was a real jungle at first, and the house was falling to pieces, but it's beginning to come together – slowly! Everything is growing now that it's May – it gives me hope instead of despair. Hope is what keeps us going, isn't it?

I've never written to anyone like this before, but if you are lonely, remember me and that I have been very lonely too. I know you can get through this – you can get through anything at all if there is just one other person in the world who believes you.

I realise that you might not want to, but I wondered if you'd like us to write to each other? I would like to write to you because although Lotte and Deanne are great, they aren't the same age as me. And I've always liked writing, ever since I was a kid.

Anyway, I'd love to hear from you – I hope you'll write back.

Yours sincerely,
Gail

I didn't show Gail's letter to anyone, though, of course, all our letters are read before we get them. I knew when I read it that it was going to change me, because it was so honest. I'd been surrounded by liars and cheats on the market, and in the prison there were only a few women I could trust – it does that to you, prison. You have to watch out for yourself 'cos no one else will. So I wrote back and told Gail, yes, why not?

Within a few days another letter arrived.

Dear Tracey,

I was so glad to hear from you. I couldn't get you out of my mind, although I tried because I was scared of you rejecting me – I've been rejected by so many people before.

I've got so much to tell you. I've never written to a stranger before, but I have written *as* a stranger. I remember at school, all they wanted us to write was nice stories about happy families. I mean, in this day and age, teachers should know better, shouldn't they? One in particular kept going on about mums and dads. Well I've told you about my experience of family life with my mum and her boyfriends, and I couldn't very well write about that. So I invented a happy scenario for myself, complete with smiling parents and pets. It got me A grades.

When I was nine, we changed teachers. By then I'd been lying to the school for a year. The new teacher was wonderful – she taught us all about literature and read to us from incredible books. She also taught us poetry and how to read it aloud. I can still remember the words of WW Gibson's 'The Ice Cart' and John Masefield's 'Cargoes' by heart. The teacher taught us those for rhythm, she said. She inspired me.

We expanded our word power dramatically and that's when I became really interested in writing. But Mum went ape – she said there was no way she was going to support me all the way to A Levels and that as soon as I turned sixteen, I would have to leave school and get a job. I knew she meant what she said. That was the year I knifed Mum's boyfriend. So I stopped going to school. I was only ten.

I never did go back to school. I stayed at home making up stories, writing lies. Inside me I was screaming – but no one knew. I used to dream of killing Mum and her boyfriends, so I made up gory cop stories and whodunnits.

70

I couldn't face school at all – I was certain somebody would see through all my pretence and would put me away. I was sent to a psychiatrist, a children's one who specialised in school phobia and he organised for me to have a home tutor. She was fantastic – Mrs Wellington – and she encouraged me to write. She also lent me lots of books, especially autobiographies and fiction.

I've been writing fiction all my life. Until now. I think this is my first truthful piece.

I hope that you are staying strong and that someone is looking after you in there. You hear a lot of things about women in prison these days. But there is no such thing as a person in prison who doesn't need a friend outside. Not even the ones who seem as hard as nails. I believe that, anyway.

I hope one day I'll meet you and we can talk properly. Write soon.

Yours sincerely,
Gail

Gail's letter really had me choked up – it was so brave of her to risk me trashing her, telling me everything like that, all her personal business. There was no way I was going to hurt her. I wrote straight back.

Dear Gail,

Thank you for your letter – it's so honest, does me good to read it. Send me a recent photo, please. I haven't got one to send you but I will tell you what I look like. Deanne and Lotte only have pictures of me when I was little.

I'm quite thin, like my mum, and my hair is dark chestnut and very short. I am five foot five and my body is very strong from all the lifting and carrying on the market. My teeth are a bit wonky, but all right. I won a competition when I was five for the girl with the nicest smile. It still works. I use it when I need to.

I've got one tattoo with a bird on it on my left shoulder, not very big, just two inches across. That was enough – it hurt like hell.

I'm all right, I think. I'm pretty tough. You have to be, don't you, just to survive. Anyhow, I've got someone who looks out for me in here.

I would love to have told Gail about Sylve but I didn't want to let them know. Sylve has a lot of experience but she won't let me touch her. I miss that, but that's the way it is. She knows exactly what to do with my body. I don't have to fake it, though I would've if I'd had to. You have to survive in here somehow. They call this the married quarters – there's a lot of it going on.

I hate being trapped in here. I hate everything about being in a cage. The smell of shit and disinfectant. The awful, awful noises of women crying or screaming. Shouting. The whole bloody caboodle.

Then, in the middle of all of that, your letter flies in through my window like a wild kestrel. When I read it I can see wild places and high moorlands like in *Wuthering Heights*. We had this one English teacher at school who used to read to us. She was such a good reader, she had us spellbound. She was really tough. We didn't give her any shit, at all. She read to us about Catherine on the moors, sobbing into her pillow and tearing it apart, taking out all the feathers. This one's a curlew, this one's a lapwing.

Your letter made me fly. It made my soul fly. I'd forgotten I had a soul at all.

Then I thought of Mum's friend, Esther. I remembered that she liked writing too. Have you ever had a letter from her? She writes to me in here and she came to see me before she left for America. I thought that was really good of her. She said something that surprised me a lot.

'I wasn't there for you when you came out. I'm so sorry, Tracey. I was full of self-doubt. I was afraid of coming out myself, so I couldn't support you.'

Honestly, Gail, she really took my breath away saying 'sorry' like that. I'm not used to the older generation being able to say sorry. I'm not much used to anyone at all saying sorry, come to that. If only Maxie had said 'sorry' I could've dealt with it all a bit better.

It was peculiar seeing Esther. She's changed. People do change, don't they? She's not as heavy on right and wrong as she used to be. She used to gallop off with her ideas without stopping to listen. She'd get right up on her soap box and off she went. She meant well, her and her generation. But times change and everything's different now. P'raps she's had to become a bit more mellow. She got herself in some shit lately, when she fell for Phoebe, Isobel's ex-lover. I 'spect that's what it is.

It can't have been easy for them older ones, can it? Do you think we take it all for granted? Esther laughed a lot and said she'd always been a stroppy cow and was proud of it, and she still believes in the F word – feminism. She asked me what I thought about all that but I closed up and said I didn't know. I think that hurt her a bit but I didn't mean to. So then I said I was glad they'd all made a women's movement and stuff like that and I think she was pleased. Her generation had to make it all up as they went along. How can anyone of that age see things from where we stand? I can't imagine being forty. That's zimmer frame country, that is!

I think that's part of my problem with Mum. She's so stubborn sometimes. But I still wish she'd come and see me. Esther wrote to say she asked Mum to soften up, but I don't know if she will.

Sally came. That was nice. She told Mum she was going up the West End shopping, so Mum had Billie, the baby.

I never wrote a letter as long as this in my life.

Write soon.

Bye for now,
Tracey

Lotte
Summer, 1988

Time passed, and our friends became used to Gail's presence in our home. It was a beautiful summer and we tried not to let it be marred by the tension around Clause 28. Jean kept us posted with what was going on, and she was all keyed up because she was going to the lesbian summer school.

'You should come up for it, Lotte. There's never been anything like it.'

'It's a bit too academic for me,' I said. 'I'm not really into workshops and stuff like that.'

'Well there's something for everyone – they're showing films and everything.'

'We'll think about it,' I said kindly, not wanting to dampen her enthusiasm. 'But we've a lot on our plate at the moment, what with the house and all that.'

What I couldn't tell her was that Gail was hoping to go to a clinic in the autumn, where they specialised in ear operations. Whether she would fully regain the hearing in her left ear, we couldn't know. We wanted to spend as much time with her as possible, before her forthcoming ordeal.

Day by day, I admired her more and loved her more deeply. I know that beauty is in the eye of the beholder (I couldn't pretend to be objective), and I know that inner beauty is also about being loved, but, to me, Gail was becoming a very beautiful dyke indeed. Her body was growing fuller, because she was happy, although her early years of undernutrition would have a lasting effect. I could see that she would welcome the time when she didn't have to wear baggy jumpers to disguise her thinness.

Day by day we grew closer, she and I, and my deep compassion for the years she had spent deprived of motherlove could bring me to tears in moments of solitude.

We had slowly started to talk about Caroline, Gail's mother. I put it to Gail that if she could possibly begin to detach herself from the pain of betrayal and see that Caroline was also a victim of circumstance, perhaps it would help her to heal. I wasn't trying to justify Caroline's behaviour to Gail, not at all. I just wanted to help Gail understand why Caroline acted the way she did and to show Gail that she had no reason to blame herself.

So, as we painted and decorated upstairs that summer, I decided to let Gail in on some of my own background, in the hope that it would strengthen her. I told her that I could remember only too well the pressure on all of us as young girls to grow up and find a husband. Even in my own home where Mum had been a happy single parent, there was hidden pressure. The assumption was that it was best to get married and have children in a 'normal' family and normal meant a mother and a father. I had grown up knowing that Mum and Grammacleg really loved me, but even so I had internalised all that stuff about heterosexuality. From an early age I had picked up the idea that really, deep down, a woman without a man is a lonely woman. I was sure that Caroline would have received the same messages so that she felt she *had* to find a man, the right man, and having found one, wanted to keep him, whatever happened. Some women *were* lonely on their own, and if they had no way of knowing how wonderful it is to love women and meet women in gay groups and so forth, then they were under immense pressure to search for a man.

I was little Lotte Clegg once upon a time, looking for my handsome prince. I can hardly believe that now, not after all these years of loving Dee. But I still feel a deep compassion for the Carolines, lost in a violent world, and passing that on to their daughters. It's such a terrible nightmare to be locked into. A cage like Tracey's prison cell in Holloway. It takes incredible strength to break open that cage and not everyone is strong enough to do so. Some don't even know they are in it.

Well, that's how it seems to me now anyway, and I do feel that most women in this society have a lot of training in *not* standing up for ourselves, not surviving alone, not being glad about being strong. One way or another most of us are taught that we cannot go it alone, or manage on our own; we must find a mate and that mate must be a man. I was a strong young woman, sociable, capable of making friends easily, but I was thoroughly schooled in the art of finding a mate. I'm appalled now how easily I learned that lesson. It nearly got me killed.

So, although my anger at Caroline for making Gail suffer was intense (how could it not be?), didn't I also have a deep knowledge of the other side of the coin? Hadn't I put up with James' violence for years and years hoping it would all change, that he would 'come to his senses' and that everything would turn out all right? Like the myths say. Like the fairy tales tell us. Let down your hair, girl, and the prince will surely come.

'Are you asking me to forgive my mother?'

'No, Gail, I am not.'

'Good, because it is very hard to forgive someone who doesn't even want to say sorry.'

'Yes, that's right. I'm not asking anything. Anything at all. What I'm concerned about is the pain that is still inside you, and how me and Dee can help you deal with it.'

'I know. Do you think it's fear that keep women like my mother from understanding gay people?'

'I don't know. I hate what happened to you, Gail, and it is wonderful that you are getting strong, and making new friends. It's just that when I think of how my own fear of loneliness kept me plugged into that awful marriage, it makes me wonder if Caroline is all bad. She's probably afraid of growing old without a partner. Some women are. I don't want you to think that it was all about you. You're not to blame for any of it; not as a baby nor as a young woman. But women who stay with violent men are sometimes victims too and their children suffer accordingly – like you did.'

'What she did was awful.'

'Yes it was. She treated you very badly.'

'I'm very, very angry.'

76

'Yes, I know. Rightly so. I'm angry on your behalf. I'm angry with the man that did it, and I'm angry with Caroline too. She chose to collude in it, and that's inexcusable. And so is this society's treatment of women who are lonely, and isolated. Looking back, I'm glad I didn't get pregnant because if I'd had a child, I could have got locked into something much worse. I got out before I was killed, and I got out before I passed my suffering down the line to any children. I am thankful for that every day.'

'You don't want me to see my mother or anything do you?'

'No, not at all. Anyway, it's not my place to want things like that. It's what you feel that matters.'

'I'm so angry with Mum I don't know what to feel. All I know is that I never want to see her again. But that hurts. I always wanted her to love me, but now, not wanting to see her, not wanting to see my own mother... It's awful. But I'm glad we can talk a bit about it. That helps.'

There's no time limit on healing. You can't know, can you, how long these things are going to take or when the anger will be transformed, or when the memories will fade, or how it will all happen. Gail knew we were her friends, she trusted us, and that was enough.

However there was also the physical legacy of the violence against her, and there were no guarantees about that, either. Gail was going to need a series of operations on her ear.

This wasn't like when Vivienne, of the V&A, had an easy operation to remove a mole on her forehead. Last month this dark brown mole suddenly started to grow just below her hairline above her left eye. She kept catching it with her comb when she was doing her hair. They took her into hospital in Southampton one morning, gave her a local anaesthetic and whipped it off. They examined it, declared it was benign and that was the end of the matter. She had three fine black silk stitches till it healed, and it took five seconds to remove them afterwards. End of story.

Whereas Gail was facing hours and hours under the anaesthetic, and internal and external stitching that would take weeks to heal.

★

Meanwhile, Gail's letters to Tracey were becoming more frequent and I noticed that she danced a little when the replies came. She would make off with them hurriedly to the quiet privacy of her room, with slightly more glow to her skin, a touch more light in her eyes. She never said anything, but most young women would rather pull nails than admit to their elders who they fancy.

There were more talks about Caroline, and the meaning of mothers and daughters, as the long summer evenings continued. It was a poignant time for me. It had a bite of salt.

I remember at school how we once boiled salt water until there was nothing left on the glass dish but the sediment. We had to dip a finger in it and put it to our lips, amid jokes about it being poison. It was simply pure salt, but I didn't enjoy the taste of it, not at all.

Dreams change. Mine had. I had never had my own children but I found myself being more like a mother than an older friend to Gail. But even as we were building up a kind of mother–daughter trust, the time was evaporating rapidly. Gail would be emerging into the late summer as a young woman in her own right, making her own friends, choosing her own lovers, becoming independent of us.

It made every evening and every weekend precious, and prolonged. There were hours and hours of companionable work on the garden and buildings to bond us closely together, even as the water boiled away beneath us.

Sometimes I felt that I was walking in an Aladdin's cave of treasures with a time lock on the door. That's when I most resented Caroline. I hadn't had the chance of children, let alone the luxury of throwing one away. Caroline had seen Gail as some sort of life sentence. Doing time. Most mothers get eighteen years. I would have eighteen months, if I was lucky. All the horrid questions would reassert themselves round and round in my head. How could she? Why did she? On and on.

Then I'd go and take a huge spade and attack a derelict vegetable plot until the anger wore off. It put me in mind of back home in Densley when we would take the coal shovel and wham it hard against the sides of the coal hole, wham, blast, wham, sod it, wham I'm furious, wham damn, damn, wham, until the rage wore off.

My mum had never once rejected either me or Essie. She knew why we were sometimes angry and she let us *be* angry, ranting and whamming with the coal shovel till it wore off. She really loved us, and she would've understood my anger as Gail's healing continued. I think she was watching over me as I pounded that spade into the soil that summer. Watching and smiling. Go for it Lotte girl. Go for it.

Gail
Summer, 1988

Dear Tracey,

They've been and gone and done it – in spite of all the demos and campaigns they have passed Clause 28. Sometimes I can't believe how stupid this government can be. They seem to think that at the end of the twentieth century they can put a stop to the ways that women seek out each other as friends and lovers by not funding anything that supports them. I'm horrified. I'm absolutely horrified.

And you in there, in that awful place. There was a documentary about a women's prison on the telly last night. It was so shocking. Most of all I remember the clanging doors and the keys. The jangle of keys everywhere. I wonder if I will ever get the sound of it out of my head. I think of you all the time. I look at photos of you as a child and wonder if I'll recognise you when I come and visit.

There's not much happening here, except that we continue to work long hours on the house and the garden is coming alive before our very eyes. I think of your kestrel flying high, then swooping down to visit you. I have an idea about the kestrel, actually.

Well, there's these two old biddies, actually old dykes – they are called the V&A, some nickname that was started years ago. Really they're very kind. Pots and pots of money. They have a holiday home on Dartmoor. Anyway we're all going down there in a few weeks' time. Vivienne is going to be seventy and they are having a party at their own home near Dorchester, followed by a holiday with some of friends at the cottage. Sounds wonderful to me. There are all sorts of old stone circles and dolmens nearby. Dolmen's a new word to me, so I looked it up. It says 'a megalithic tomb consisting of uprights with a capstone. [French, possibly from Cornish, tolmen, meaning "hole of stone".]' You learn something new every day, don't you! I'll send you some photos.

I asked Dee and Lotte if you and me could have a holiday there when you come out. Then you will definitely get to see kestrels, firsthand. I hope you like the idea. The V&A have said it'd be no cost for us, none at all. You could rest there and get really tanned out in the open air again – no keys, they don't even bother to lock the door at night. And no more prison food. We'd only have to pay for the phone calls – all the rest is free to friends of the V&A. Years ago I'd have been too shy to ask for such a thing, but being friends with you makes me feel stronger each day.

I am slowly learning to trust other people because of these lovely women. It's something that takes a long time to learn – other people I mean. Dee and Lotte are different because I have always known them, but with others it is so slow. I have to get to know people really well before I can open up. But if Dee and Lotte say that the V&A are okay and won't let me down, then I believe them.

Well I must go now. I am thinking of you all the time.

Your new friend,
Gail

A few days later I received her reply.

Dear Gail,

Oh yes, I would love to go to Dartmoor. I can't wait to see the big skies and wild open places. I try to imagine it when I'm lying here in my bunk, after lights out. I try to think of the peace and quiet. Mum used to say that when she was evacuated to Penny Acre Farm during the war she couldn't sleep because of the quiet. She'd rather listen out for feet on the stone balconies outside the old flats in London, and traffic in the streets and the noises of other people all around. I think she was frightened in the country till she got used to it.

Here it is never quiet. Sounds of metal and stone, tiles and pipes, cisterns and lavatories, tubes and stairways. Doors clanging. Yes, you're right about the doors. I am so miserable here that I just go from day to day. It's okay with Sylve. I let her do anything she wants. So it works all right. She's the boss. No question 'bout it.

I like what you said 'bout trusting Dee and Lotte. I don't trust anyone. 'Cept myself. I trust myself to get through this. And when I think I can't do another day of it, then I just do an hour, or get through to the next meal (even though it is prison muck). This is the hardest thing I have *ever* done in my life.

I don't know how they think this is going to make me a better person. Well, how can being banged up make you anything but wild and angry? That's the question I keep asking myself. How can this make me full of remorse, or go to church, or get Jesus for my friend, or all that crap, *huh*? The ones who run this place will never get inside my head.

Some suited grey-haired nob in the Home Office starts spouting garbage about reform of the prisons. Or is it the civil servants? The ones who design the whole fucking system. They've probably been to Oxford or some such shit, and got their heads all fucked up with philosophy and policies. I bet not one of them ever worked in Tesco all summer – bet they took off round India on 'Daddy's money' or shit like that. They don't know what ordinary people are like. They haven't worked down Lewisham market that's for sure.

Me, I love the open air and I can hardly wait for that time on Dartmoor. Send me some pictures whenever you can and maybe a guide book or three. I need stuff to look at. Nothing heavy. There's too much noise here for anything heavy. I think about hearing wild water pounding down the rocks. I want to watch the wind making the grass into waves like the sea. I will hold on to it, Gail. I will hold on to the hope of it.

So I must go now.

It's a day at a time. It feels like for ever.

There's an awful lot of days in for ever.

Your friend,
Tracey

Deanne
Early September, 1988

The first weekend of September we began to clear the brambles from a wild garden which lay to the right of the orchard. I had noticed that there were tall straggly branches with recognisable leaves showing through the tangle and I was curious as to what lay behind there.

I worked with Gail all that weekend, cutting the brambles into neat lengths before removing them with very thick gloves. Lotte was in Paris, working overtime for her legal firm because they had a major libel case to prepare. Once or twice a year she'd be called upon to go abroad with her boss, and we needed the money.

Back at Mere Cottage we couldn't work very fast because it was like unravelling barbed wire, so intricately were the strands intertwined. We slogged all Saturday and Sunday, inching forwards. I'd been right about the redcurrant bushes. We pruned them as we found them, and I carried the prunings across to the nursery beds and pushed them one by one into a freshly dug trench, hoping that my cuttings would produce a new row of young bushes.

Returning to the wild patch, we worked steadily, trying to make an inroad into the jungle-like growth. We talked of the power of transformation and how the gardening that we were sharing was a reflection of our lives.

'It's like I'm untangling the past and making a path to the future here, doing this work,' said Gail.

'It takes some untangling, sometimes.'

'I was reading Esther's entries in the book you made, *Three Ply*

Yarn. She said she wanted a "warp thread strong enough to dance on".'

'You have to have the threads ready first, don't you?'

'Yes, going right forward, stretching ahead of you. Carrying you into the future. I don't want to dwell on the past. But my future, that's a different matter. It's an open book. When I was younger, I thought I'd like to be a writer. It's just a hobby now, but I love the idea of all the blank pages in my diary. My life ahead of me.' She smiled hugely at me, and we bent over our work.

We were aware of the season turning during that weekend. Some of the brambles had their first scarlet leaves, and the slant of the sun over the South Downs was altering rapidly. It made a remarkable difference to the light in the garden. I'd always noticed that the movement of the sun is at its fastest as the time draws near to one of the equinoxes. Esther intended to go with her women's group north to Oregon for a celebration, for the festival of equal night and day. I was glad that she had found something special but I didn't want her spirituality for myself – I had my own quiet way of noting the annual cycle because I was a gardener. I felt that the land had a strong sense of spirit, but that was enough for me.

Lotte returned from France and we took the next day off. I woke early that morning, sensing a hint of autumn in the air. There comes one particular morning, each year, when the summer has finished. There's not much dramatic change in the weather but I just know it, feel it, as if there is in the air the taste of Worcester apples.

I woke slowly, and lay quietly in the half light, listening to Lotte's steady breathing. It took me back to that first quiet morning in 23 Station Road, when I had woken beside her after our first night together. I was forty-five and she, twenty-nine, and I had woken astonished and delighted to find love in my life once again.

I crept out of bed without waking her and padded out of our bedroom, closing the door gently behind me. I'd stopped smoking years ago, and instead of making a roll-up, I made fresh coffee and buttered toast which I ate hungrily. I'm always very hungry the morning after sex with Lotte.

Then I pulled on my gardening jacket over my pyjamas, changed my slippers for thick socks and wellies, and carried my second steaming mug of coffee outside. A low autumnal mist was evaporating off the grass. There were autumn crocuses under the trees near our picnic table, a *prunus autumnalis* was now in delicate pink flower, contrasting perfectly with its purplish leaves, and birdsong echoed in the early morning air. I stood absolutely still, listening to the sounds of the garden. There was distant traffic on its way to Brighton. You can't avoid that in East Sussex. I didn't mind. It was a long way off and it didn't interfere with my gentle, balanced mood.

It was so many years since my first awakening with Lotte, in that tiny house in Station Road. We were like two bookends now, a bit dusty, either end of a shelf of stories. None of them boring; all of them easy to read.

I walked along the viburnum path, through its twists and turns, realising that its autumn flowers were in full bud, some even had tiny flowers already. I came to the orchard and sat down on a new wooden seat made by Gail in August. Looking back towards the house I saw the first yellow leaves on the cherry tree, and one crimson one, much too early. They don't usually turn till November.

My reverie over, I wandered through the orchard checking the summer growth on each tree, planning the forthcoming sessions of pruning. Last year we had been quite ruthless but it seemed to be paying off, and there was no sign of disease. We had some old varieties of Victorian apples, so someone at some time had been specialising here, though the oldest trees were only about thirty. Fruit trees don't last very long in any case.

Something led me to the wild patch where Gail and I would be slogging after breakfast. I stood beside the currant bushes, looking inwards, and realised that the roof of the garden, as it's called, was not a continuous slope nor did it have a flat top. I moved back to the orchard wall and climbed up, muddying my pyjamas in the process. Holding on to an overhanging apple branch I surveyed the wild patch.

From my new height I could gain perspective. I had been right, the top of the wild patch was not continuous. It dipped as if the land beneath it also dipped and the tangled brambles seemed to follow the outline of a building or an old roofless shed of some kind. I couldn't make out any details at all, just a vague shape suggesting a rectangle.

I regarded it for a long while until the rising sun had cleared all the mist. If there was a building under there it was ruined and there was no way to tell, from my vantage point, what it had been.

Laughing to myself, I scrambled back down from the orchard wall and made my way towards the house, humming merrily. Halfway along the garden I was drawn onwards by the smell of fresh coffee and croissants. Lotte and Gail were up and dressed in their gardening gear, ready for the morning's work.

'I've found a building,' I said, excitedly.

'Where? In the wild patch?'

'Yes, you can just make out an oblong shape.'

'You'll eat first, won't you, love?' Lotte came and kissed me.

'Well just a bite – I've already had some toast and I'm raring to go.' I went round to hug Gail who was tucking into eggs and toast.

'Mmmm,' she said, her mouth full, 'Morning Dee. You were up early.'

'It's beautiful out there. Can't wait to get going.'

We spent the morning, until Lotte and Gail insisted we break for a late lunch, hacking at brambles until we had reached a series of brick steps leading down.

'So why did they plant redcurrants here, near some steps?' Lotte asked.

'Dunno. Maybe they just wanted a working garden.'

'Maybe we'll find an old chest with treasure in it.'

'You said that when we opened up the attic!'

We all laughed and continued clipping and pulling, strand by strand, each one vicious with needle-sharp thorns.

'There's brick under here. Come and clear this bit with me,' said Gail.

'Yes, and look,' I said scraping at the soil, 'there's some tiling. Some sort of conservatory.'

'It's going to take hours, but I'm sure you're right. This is a lovely pattern.'

So we worked on, past tea time, until dusk.

It was an old conservatory, complete with rotten wooden chairs and a table. By Monday night we'd hacked our way inside and had a sense of its size. It had been about sixteen foot long and eight foot wide, with a glass roof. The roof had fallen in together with the glass and the wooden frames of the walls. But over the next two weekends we revealed a lovely brick floor, in herring-bone pattern, like the ones found in the outbuildings of Victorian estates all over the country.

'This must've been part of the gardens of a big estate,' said Lotte.

'So our house wasn't farm workers' cottages?'

'No, p'rhaps not. Maybe they were gardeners' houses, part of the workforce on the estate. I mean, they had a fair number of people to feed on those estates, didn't they. They grew every-thing, to feed the servants and all. It's beautiful, isn't it, even if it's derelict.'

The doorway had faced east, which surprised us, because the east winds can be fierce in the winter. The whole thing was covered in honeysuckle, brambles, and one or two remaining old roses. The bricks were higgledy-piggledy on the floor, tilted at different angles where ferns and brambles were growing up underneath.

Gail went out with her camera and recorded each stage of the unravelling. When we asked her why she was taking so much care over the photos she said, 'Because I'd like to rebuild it, and we wouldn't want the planners asking questions about what's going on – it's simply what was there before. I'd like to restore it to its former glory, herringbone floors and all!'

Gail
Early September, 1988

Lotte and Dee were out in the garden again, clearing more brambles from the windbreak hedges that surround the vegetable plot. We'd had fantastic salads all summer, so it had been worth the effort. They were both still working full time in their jobs in Brighton, so it only left evenings and weekends for the garden. Now we were all making the most of the hours of daylight before the autumn began to close in. I boiled the kettle and carried the mugs out with some chocolate chip cookies on a tray.

'Thought you might like a tea break,' I said, smiling at them. 'You both look so dirty. You're unbelievable!'

Lotte wiped her nose on her sleeve, ruefully, and Dee emerged covered in bramble scratches and smudges of soil.

We sprawled on the grass, munching and drinking. I decided to broach the subject on my mind.

'You know I've been writing to Tracey? Well she's made me think a lot about friendship and I've decided I'd like to visit her in prison. What do you think?'

'It'd be good for you to meet,' said Lotte, thoughtfully. 'But are you sure you're ready for that place, for seeing her there in prison?'

'I think so. Ready as I'll ever be. The thing is Stuart is going up to London in a little while and he said he'd take me and bring me back. I could say I was her cousin visiting. She writes to me every week now and I thought I'd like to visit her before I go to the clinic. See her face to face.'

'You didn't need to ask us,' replied Lotte, 'you can go wherever you like, you know that.'

'I know, but I might be in a bit of a state if it doesn't work out very well. That's why I wanted you to know all about it. Okay?'

'Fine by us,' said Lotte. 'Isn't it Dee?'

'Yes, of course. We'll be here when you get back. Actually it's a good idea that you meet Tracey because you're probably going to meet her mother, Nell, soon,' Dee added.

'Yes, it's come as a bit of a surprise to us, but Nell has been invited to Vivienne's seventieth.'

'Nell? Why? I mean how come she knows the V&A?'

'Through the holiday cottage,' replied Dee. 'Years ago when Nell was ill they loaned it to her for a convalescence. They met her there and saw her settled in. They all got along like a house on fire.'

Lotte took up the story with, 'So we could, if you like, meet her here before we all go to Vivienne's do. We thought of asking her down because she's not seen this place yet, what with Billie and everything. And I think she wants to patch things up with Tracey, so you wouldn't have that hanging over you.'

'Yes. But I think Tracey's not so angry with her any more either. It's better that they're getting everything out in the open. Made me do some serious thinking. I want to tell Tracey everything when I see her – the whole story. And I don't mind if Nell knows either. The thing is, I'm getting stronger all the time now. I'm facing a lot of facts. I don't want any more secrets. It's no shame that my mum's boyfriend swiped me. And Nell is your oldest friend and you're my new family. Besides, it's not long till Vivienne's, and if Nell's been invited, I'll get to meet her there anyway. The party's just the right timing for me – just before my clinic sessions.'

'Yes, it is good timing, for once! Anyway, when Vivienne rang us she said that Nell's been keeping in touch since that visit to the holiday cottage, and they thought she could do with a break on her own after caring for Billie like she does. She's going to leave Billie with Fred; so she can have a complete change and a rest as well. We were a bit surprised to tell you the truth, but that's Nell for you – you never know where she's going to turn up! She is such good fun at a party, she'll be the life and soul of it down on Dartmoor, you mark my words.'

Lotte laughed, 'I think she's been invited as the honorary straight actually. She'll be surrounded by spinsters.'

'You're not exactly a spinster, Lotte.'

'No, more's the pity. Though I am an excellent knitter and I can spin many a good yarn. Anyway, if my sister Esther is anything to go by, a spinster is an independent woman without a man, and proud to be so. So that definitely counts me in.'

'I give in. I give in. You can be a spinster, okay?'

We were all laughing by then. Poor Lotte was so determined not to be classified with Nell as the token straight, and anyway, she hadn't been straight for donkey's years by then. But it set me to thinking about lesbians and history, and how in the past so many lesbians had to tell lies or hide their family life in some way. And how, even now, young lesbians can get thrown out of their homes just for wanting to be themselves.

I thought how incredibly lucky I was to have new lesbian 'parents'. I decided I'd look at the books of coming out stories and lesbian poetry that Lotte liked to read, since she first discovered that she loved women, well, one woman in particular. As I watched them teasing each other, I suddenly felt older than both of them put together and loved them so much that it brought a lump to my throat.

Nell
September, 1988

I went to see my Trace last week. It was awful in there. All those women, hours and hours on end in their cells, not enough activity. Not enough exercise.

But it's no good waiting to get old and sick and losing my girls is it? I only got one crack at this life and if I lose my Tracey, well, what's the point of it all?

So I went to see her, in that place.

She says to me, 'What made you change your mind, then, Mum?'

I says, 'It was our Sally getting sick in August what did it. She was so ill, throwing up for four days. Put me in mind of my Mum when she died of cancer of the colon. Really put the wind up me, it did. I know it was silly. It was only four days, then she was right as rain. But you know, when somethin' clicks inside you, and you change? Like when the hand jumps on the station clock? You're watching it, and it's ticking away. Then suddenly it jumps, just like that, to the next number? Well, my brain did that. Sally was so ill, and suddenly I saw me mother, "Hannah, wot carries the banner", ill and dying. And I thought, "What if I lose my girls? What if something happens to my Trace and I can't ever tell her she's mine, and I love her?" I can't lose my girls. I can't. Life's too short. So I thought, even if them drugs was my Tracey's she's still my daughter. I've got to go and see her. So I've come. I'm that glad to see you, Tracey.'

She's tough as old boots, my Trace, what with her tattoo and her women lovers and all. And her short hair. *And* she smokes. Smoking herself to death, she is. But, she was sat there trying not to cry. Right in front of everybody, just because her mum'd come to see her.

She says, 'They weren't mine. I swear it. You've got to believe me, Mum.'

I was sat opposite her. There were warders all round the walls. Holding up the walls, they was. What did they think I was going to get up to? Do a runner with me daughter?

I sat there and watched my Tracey gulping and trying not to show tears and I said, 'I know, Trace. I know they wasn't. I do believe you.'

Prisons is my thing now. There should be a real hoohah about the women's prisons. Women are sent down for petty crimes. Crimes of debt. It's *Little Dorrit* again. I did weep over that film. I thought them days was long gone, but they're not. They're right here on my doorstep.

Well, I haven't had a campaign since Esther was at Reeve Juniors and we did the After School Play Club. I've done a few meetings for this and that – the school crossing and the lollipop ladies being cut, stuff like that. I did courses on Aids and courses about looking after blind children because Sally's friend Marianne Mackintosh had a little blind baby, Sophie. But I haven't had nothing special to fight for, not till I went to see my Tracey in prison.

This isn't history, you know. This is now. Women in prison because they can't pay the bills. Crimes that only poor people commit. This is no way to run the country. There's politicians creaming it off from companies, and businessmen with assets all over the shop and nothing happens. Then some woman on the social steps out of line and wham, they throws the book at her.

My Sally's been prison visiting. My Sally's been all over. On account of her bloke Earl's friends. I says to her, 'Some folks travels where the tourism is, some folks go where the galleries is, and you my girl, you know where all the blokes' prisons is.'

What a way to see the country.

Sally has a job now. Tuesdays, Thursdays, Saturdays, ten till four. She's in a charity shop. Says it's very sociable and if they won't let her work in a proper job while she's a single mum, she might as well do the charity shop. Gets her out of the house.

She takes Billie with her. I never thought she'd stick it. I admire her grit.

Me, I get around a bit now that I have met Christopher. His mates call him Chris, but I love his full name. It sets him apart. To me, he is set apart. He is nothing to do with Reeve Green, the pan, the play club, fundraising, campaigns, or prisons. He is to do with me, and the rest of my life is set apart from what I do with him.

With Christopher I do the galleries. And the museums. We do the world of art and culture. I love him for it.

Ess wrote to me: 'Going to the galleries? Is that what you do because you and Christopher need somewhere to go, Nell?'

I put her right about that. Does she think that people like me can't enjoy paintings? I love the galleries. I could look at art for hours and hours. It's what me and Christopher share. Something we can talk about. We chat away and my arm's linked in his and it's wonderful.

It's been four years now since he first asked me out. I heard my mum's voice, 'Be careful Nell. It never stops at two drinks.'

It never does, does it? But I went anyway.

He came into our office to mend the phones. Then he came regularly for the new switchboards. They're fast, the new boards. I can't phone Deanne now, because it's all logged. No outside calls. I still work the late shift, three till seven. It suits me, and the money's good.

I had to take Fred to the solicitors – not Slomners, I keep Fred and Slomners well apart – and they drew up a list. What he pays for and what I pay for. He's still hoping to play a system for the geegees but most of them have three legs. He wins sometimes but then he loses it all again. We muddle along all right and there's no rows now over money. He hands over what he has to pay, usually. He's better since Billie came along. He'll pay his half to keep a roof over Billie's head, not mine.

I like to dine out with my Christopher. He can afford it and I don't ask questions.

He said once that he was ready to leave his wife for me. But I couldn't leave Billie. I could no more walk off into the sunset with Christopher than fly. So it suits us both and I look forward to my awaydays. Not very often, just now and then.

Friday nights is my time with Christopher. He meets me from work and we walk arm in arm to the pictures, or a restaurant. It's magic and I didn't expect it. I always come home at half past ten. Fred says nothing. He doesn't want to know. But he must know, he couldn't not know. Fred's not stupid.

Fred doesn't want much from me. We still do sex from time to time. He's good at it. He always was. It's all right. I keep him happy. Keep the honey pot sweet. That's how to survive.

I thought about the past few years through the whole train journey to Brighton. It was my first visit to Mere Cottage. I'd've liked to come before now but they got Gail and I thought maybe she was a bit of a tearaway 'cos they kept saying they wanted to give her time to settle down.

When I was all packed and ready, I says to 'im indoors, 'Right. I'm off then. You be all right with Billie?'

The floor dweller looks up at me from his place on the carpet, surrounded by copies of the *Sporting Life*. He's doing form. He says, ''Course I will. I'll take her to the park in the buggy. Feed the ducks.'

'It's September, right? Make sure she's wrapped up warm won't you, Fred?'

He smiles at me as if I'm senile.

'Go on, Nell. Stop fussing. She's the apple of my eye, my granddaughter. She'll be all right with me. After the park, I'll take her down the betting shop.'

What can you say? He was as good as gold with our girls. He didn't love me, he didn't know how to, and he's a complete no-hoper, is my Fred, but he is very gentle. Never laid a hand on my girls. Took them everywhere with him, bless him. Took them to the geegees. Took them to the dogs. My Tracey could fill in a betting slip, age six. That's how she learned to count.

So I got myself to East Croydon station, and caught the

Brighton train, and all the time there was Billie on my mind. I was still back in the time when Billie was first born. I knew from the start that my Sally couldn't go it alone. So I didn't like to leave Billie for very long, not when she was first born. Then later I was in a right two and eight after she fell down the stairs at Tracey's flat. I fretted for ages. It really put the wind up me. So it had suited me to stay in Reeve Green, not go galavanting off to Mere Cottage. It took me nearly the whole train journey to settle my mind, because it was the first time I had left my granddaughter to give myself a holiday.

Dee showed me round the house which was done up lovely, though not finished – it'll take years. We put my bag in my room, had lunch, then we walked all around the garden.

We started at the far side, just through the arch around the corner where they found the old potato plots and the strawberries. There was purple sprouting broccoli growing – I do like a bit of broccoli with me Sunday roast, but it's too expensive at home now because my Trace can't get it free off the market no more.

Then we went into the orchard. Very old trees. Nice. I liked the orchard. Then down the viburnum walk, as they call it. It's this romantic winding path with bushes with flowering tops on, like tiny bouquets, the sort bridesmaids hold. Pink they were, stuck on the end of leafy branches. Some were out, some still in bud.

'You want pink bridesmaids and the Wedding March along here.'

We all laughed. It was a lovely, lovely garden. Secret nooks and crannies everywhere. And some still wild and tangled.

At the far end you could climb on to a stone seat and look over a wall, and there was farmers' fields right up on to the Downs.

I turned to Deanne who was shining with it. The whole place put me in mind of the farm, Penny Acre Farm, where we was evacuated in the war. I smiled at Dee and told her what I was thinking.

'We go back a long way, Nell,' she said. Which was true.

*

Back indoors they began to tell what had happened to Gail. Said Gail wanted me to know. It was a long and all too familiar story.

Lotte finished, 'In my opinion, if Gail had married Terry and left home, Caroline would've heaved a sigh of relief and washed her hands of her. I feel she just wanted rid of motherhood. It'd tie in with her telling Gail she wouldn't keep her after she was sixteen anyway, wouldn't see her through A Levels, didn't have to keep a roof over her daughter's head after that.'

'Oh my God. Oh, Jeez, that's what I did to my Tracey. All them years ago when she came out and left home. Oh, Jeez.'

'You've made your peace with Tracey,' said Dee. 'You've been to see her in prison. It's different, Nell. It's going to be all right.'

'Oh I hope so. I treated her bad when she came out. I told her I was sorry.'

'She knows that now.'

'I hope so, I really do. Tell you what. I'm more glad than ever I been to see her. I wasn't there for her when she needed me, when she left school and came out. But, I never hated my child. I wanted her and she was loved. But I failed her when she was in her teens and what you're saying to me now about Gail, well it chokes me. Why can't we just accept our kids the way they are? Why do we set 'em up, give 'em such a hard time, when all they want is to be loved?'

Dee said, 'I don't know, Nell. But you have been to see Tracey – it *is* different.'

'Good.'

Lotte said, gently, 'Gail's making a new life, now. She's much better in herself. And she's made friends with Tracey. Wants to visit her, in prison. She's come out to us, but not to the whole world. It's too soon, yet.'

'That's why she chose to live with you?' I sighed. 'She's lucky to have you two to turn to. I wish my Trace had been so lucky. I failed her so many times. I don't know why. I expect it's because she's too much like me. She winds me up. But I do love her.'

The end of a long day. My first day at Mere Cottage. Standin' by the bedroom window, looking out, just thinkin' about friends. No street lights here. It's a dark night. I'm glad Dee's happy. If you'd known her, as I did, in Rotherhithe before the war, you'd know what it means to me to see her settled with Lotte, safe and housed like this. We go back a long, long way, me and Deanne Derby. Friends for ever. Dee's known me all my life, no secrets, no excuses. Friends like that, you're lucky if you can count them on the fingers of one hand.

Look at all them stars. My Tracey can't see the night sky from in there. All banged up behind bars. I hope you know I'm thinking about you, Tracey. Because I am. And I may not be the best mum you could've had, but I am your mum, and you was not a mistake. Me and Fred, we wanted you. Your Gran never saw you – she'd have loved you, you look a bit like her, when she was young. I do love you.

It's a cold night. No clouds. I hope Billie's got her warm pyjamas on. Good night Billie. Sweet dreams. Nanny will be home soon.

Tracey
September, 1988

Gail is my friend now. She writes to me between visits. Helps me stay sane. It's an insane place. The whole fucking system's insane. Terrible things go on. Pregnant women shackled to their beds when they've got to go to hospital . . . It's a bloody nightmare.

I'm really looking forward to Gail's next visit. Won't be for a while. There's Vivienne's party, then Gail has to have the ear operations. I don't envy her that.

I write to three women now – Gail, Rebecca and Esther in San Francisco. Their letters keep me going.

This is what I wrote.

Dear Rebecca,

Thank you for your letter. I think about your kestrel. Last night, I lay in my bunk, eyes open, in the dark, and I could feel its wings, picture it flying in my mind's eye. It's peaceful, flying high. No one can catch it, or hurt it. It helps me.

Peaceful. I think about that word a lot. There's no peace in here. That's your job isn't it, making peace. That's why you ended up in here.

Mum came to see me. I've had just one visit from her so far. We made peace. She's away right now staying with her friends, Dee and Lotte, down near Brighton. She has known Dee all her life, that's fifty-four years. But what really bonded them to start with was not peace. It was war. They were evacuees together.

Dee and Lotte are the ones who've offered to let me stay with them when I get out of here.

In one of your letters, you said that peace was your dream for the whole world. Is it still?

My dream is to be free. To get out of here.

Bye for now,
Tracey

Dear Tracey,

Yes, peace is my dream for the whole world, but when I was at Greenham I just put all my energies into that one campaign – you have to start somewhere.

I was glad to hear that you have been offered a place to stay when you leave prison. I too have been lucky, and now share a house with three women friends in Leeds.

I have returned to my studies and there are quite a few mature students so I don't feel out of place. It's not easy trying to get a degree in my thirties, but I am enjoying the courses very much indeed – sociology and some women's studies. I'm catching up on my reading, though I still struggle a bit with my long essays.

The kestrel that came to me in prison was real – it was the spirit of a young kestrel from my childhood which was spent in the village of Oxenhope, not far from the Brontë parsonage at Howarth. Up on the moors the skies are high and wide.

My sister still lives there and I'm sure she would put you and your friend Gail up for free. She does that sort of thing as a way of supporting women in prison and from Greenham – women like myself. She has a disabled daughter so she can't always get away from home though she did come down for one of the 'Embrace the Base' demos. She's more like a fairy godmother to me than a biological sister, being twelve years older than I am. Let me know if you ever want to stay with her.

Say goodnight to the kestrel for me.

Your friend,
Rebecca

A postcard came today from Esther. I'll treasure it. I read everything many times over.

Hi Tracey,

We're on our way north to Oregon and beyond, to stay with the women on Oregon Women's Land – OWL. This mountain always has a snowcapped top and was a sacred mountain from time immemorial. Will write at length on my return. We had earth tremors just before we left, nothing to worry about, very low on the Richter scale. The teacups rattled a bit on the dresser, but that's all. Love from Phoebe and myself,

Esther

I didn't wait to write back. I wrote straight away.

Dear Esther,

Thank you for your postcard.

I get letters now from you, Gail, and Rebecca from Greenham.

I was sorry to hear about the earth tremors in San Francisco. I wish you would come back home before there is a *really* serious one. Mum was right wasn't she! She said it was that sort of city. Why do you stay in a place as frightening as that? I wouldn't. But a nice little earthquake would be a good thing *here*. Just a little one – enough to shake this building so that I could walk down the roof into the street. And never look back.

I was going to write anyway this week to tell you Mum came to see me. She didn't have a lot to say, but it was all right. She had tears in her eyes. I'd been so hurt by her not believing me, and it'd made me so angry I'd planned I was going to play it cold when I met her. I don't forgive easily. But Mum's visit changed me. I could see that she was really sorry. She was genuine. I could tell. It takes a lot for someone like my mum to say she's sorry. Not a word you hear a lot from her. We made peace, and I'm glad. But I felt all churned up after she'd gone.

Then Gail came – her first visit – two firsts, one after the other. Quite something. I was very pleased to see her, and she said I was exactly like she'd imagined me. She was very bright-eyed, kind of sparkly, you know? She thought the visiting area was horrible, which it is. But even so, I could tell she was more than thrilled to be with me. Have I started something there? Dunno. Didn't mean to. I'm going to take up Dee and Lotte's offer of a room when I get out of here because it's somewhere to go. I've lost my flat and although Mum's said sorry I don't think moving back in with her would be a good idea. But I do think Gail hopes I'll be more than just a friend. That's the last thing on my mind. So I hope it doesn't get too awkward.

Gail's had a bad time and I don't want to hurt her. She *is* my friend, so I'll be kind to her. Let her down gently. There will be plenty of time to talk to her when I get out of here, won't there? Maybe she got the wrong idea because I told her that getting letters made my soul fly. But I was thinking of my kestrel; about getting out of here and being free.

Getting out of here is mainly what I think of. All the time. Being in here is like being dead while you're alive. It's dead time. Your life is ticking, like a clock. On and on. It gets to some of the women. They can't cope. They start cutting themselves up. I don't sleep when it happens. It's horrible. Pulls me right down just to think of it. Sylve says, just don't think about it and I try not to. I try to not care at all. God, what a mess this all is. Sometimes I get so low it's like I'm living under the earth with a huge weight pressing me down. But I do bounce back when letters come.

I'm glad you are happy with Phoebe – what a tangle! Somebody told me that the trouble with the women's movement is everybody is everybody's ex-lover.

Now I am waiting to hear from Gail. They are at a party near Dorchester, then they are going to Dartmoor. Lotte and Dee christened it the 'Old Maids' Knees Up', and there's something to do with a legend about some stones near the holiday cottage.

Please write soon.

One of your long letters. Please?

Love from,
Tracey

Esther
10 September, 1988

Dear Tracey,

Thank you for your letter telling me about your Mum's visit to see you. I am so glad she has come to her senses at last. I can imagine just how vulnerable it would make you feel, opening up like that to your Mum after all these months, then having to close down again to cope with the conditions you are living in. Opening and closing is never easy. I've never been in prison, but I can imagine how very hard it would be to close down again after opening up so much in my relationship with Phoebe. So, for that reason, I think of you very often and whenever the moon is full I go out on to the balcony here and watch the sky, using the moon to send strength and perseverance to you. You're a very passionate person, lively and wilful, which is good and it will see you through because you have such a determination to live life to the full. I've known you a long time and I'm sure that you can do this. You can get through it and *you will*. We are all rooting for you, Tracey, willing you to survive day by day. In your bleak moments remember that, because our spirits are with you, just like the kestrel spirit is with you and that means that your spirit is never alone.

I'm glad to hear also that your first visit from Gail went well. Yes, it is a bit scary, realising that someone is falling for you and wondering what your own feelings are. I am glad that you enjoy her friendship so much. Besides, as you rightly say, there is no hurry. There is plenty of time for you to develop the new friendship and to find out what you really want from it. I only met her once and she was still very shy, so we did not have a chance to get to know each other.

I have just come back from a trip up the coast as far as Seattle, where the women's movement is still very strong. On the way we called in to see the women of Oregon Women's Land because they have contacts in San Francisco.

I became very interested in all the different ways that women are creating women's land here in the States and hope to do some visiting in the spring and summer of next year. There are over thirty areas of women's land now but some are private and I don't know of many that are open like OWL.

I am also deeply involved in a women's spirituality group here. We are exploring ways of celebrating the Earth Mother, Gaia, and following the cycles of the year, doing ceremonies, some indoors and some outside in the summer months. I'm trying to put together my politics and my spirituality in new ways, ways that make them equal in my mind and my soul.

I was amazed to read in your letter that you are experiencing the kestrel as a soul flight, well, that's my phrase for it. You said that you didn't know you had a soul till the kestrel came along and Gail began to write to you. I never thought I had one either – it was all politics and education for me right through the years till I did the book with Dee and Lotte. Then I did some research on the spinning and weaving Goddesses. But it didn't really connect with me at soul level – for me it was more about history and discovering role models for women.

Then I met Phoebe and maybe it was falling in love with her that finally set my soul free to fly. I'm not sure exactly what the sequence of events was that brought me to where I am now. A combination of things, probably.

I also have a strong sense of spirit, spirit in all natural things, especially when I am by the huge ocean here, and when I have a chance to leave the city and go to the redwoods. They are so tall, stretching up to an infinite sky and connecting down almost to the centre of the earth. I feel their spirits very strongly and I stand quietly in the forest touching them and feeling absolutely at peace.

104

My group does a circle before our ceremonies calling up the four directions, and the spirits that represent them. I love the moment when the circle is cast, and the ceremony is about to begin. I feel complete, whole, excited, and very grounded. Our group tends to follow the European tradition of the four elements of air, fire, water, and earth being east, south, west, and north respectively. The Native American women do this quite differently. I have two friends here who call in the thunder spirits, which feels amazing when we do ceremonies together.

I am deeply happy these days, happier than I can ever remember being in my life, and healing from the trauma of little Josie Brown's death. At last the pain is easing off, and the nightmares are subsiding. I think you are right to say that it will take you a long time to get over what you are experiencing now, Tracey, but you will heal, given time.

There is something I thought of, though it might not help, but I will say it anyway.

Even in a place like prison, the water that flows through the showers comes originally from the rain, and the rivers that feed the reservoirs. Your kestrel flies over them, and witnesses this process while it is happening.

Every time you take a shower you can connect with the living waters of the earth. It may only be two or three minutes, in the most appalling place you can think of, but it is the same water and you can use it to help you to heal; and to stay strong.

Many urban women, living like I do in the city, have nowhere to go to honour and celebrate the Earth Mother, so they refresh their souls in whatever little ways they can. I have a friend who does her water rituals under the surface of the swimming pool near where she lives. Her name is Barbara. She insists that city women can be very spiritual – you don't have to be in a lonely place in the wild to connect with the Earth Mother. 'She' is in every stone and brick, in every building – the Earth Mother is in the city, because her body is the city itself, made by people from her own resources, stone, concrete, wood, glass and metal. Isn't that an amazing thought?

The bed you are sleeping on has a metal frame. I was

researching the gift of metal recently, and came upon the great Goddess of Ireland, Bride. (They pronounce her name Breed.)

She was the Great Mother of all Ireland, a fire Goddess who appeared to her people in her triple aspect: she was Goddess of the healing waters and holy wells; Goddess of poetry and foretelling of the future; and Goddess of smithcraft who taught her people the gift of working metal. She is a healing Goddess and protector, and will always come when you call. She understands your need, your despair, your loneliness, and is there to comfort you even in your bleakest moments. She will never forsake you, even though human beings will let you down and have done in the past, including myself.

There is a wonderful twist to this research which will perhaps amuse you. When Christianity came to Ireland, Bride eventually became St Bridget. It's hardly possible to separate out whether the saint was also the abbess, Bridget of Kildare or whether they were two separate women. No matter. There is evidence that the abbess was in a relationship with one of her religious colleagues, another woman. Well, with all that female spirituality it makes perfect sense to me! Thought you'd like that little gem!

I don't know if any of this is of any comfort to you, but I have enjoyed writing this letter, and will continue with my reading and research in the hope of writing more in the future. I suppose what I am really trying to say is that there are many of us who really care about you, how you are every day, and every night, willing you to have more days that are do-able than days that are not, willing you to know, *really* know that our spirits are connected with yours.

Whenever I used to be asked what I meant by politics, I used to say that it was the study of the distribution of power. I haven't left any of that urgent study behind me; it lives in every molecule of my body. I have heard it labelled a new way in the States. Here somebody political is said to have 'attitude'. So, the women in my group talk about 'spirituality with attitude'.

What does that mean to me, Esther Clegg? It means that I want them to stop hunting down the kestrels. To let the wild things of the earth fly free so that their spirits can soar.

That is why I need to go on challenging who has the power, who runs the institutions, who puts all these women in prison. I know that you have spirit, and that you won't let anyone kill it. 'You can't kill the spirit. It is like a mountain. Tall and strong. It goes on and on and on.'

You can do it, Tracey. A day at a time.

Love,
Esther

Gail
September, 1988

The Froggery
Dorchester

Dear Tracey,

We arrived here at Viv and Amy's place about five in the evening, with a couple of hours to go before sunset. The garden was ablaze with autumn flowers, dahlias of all colours, huge chrysanthemums and the remainder of summer's large white daisies. It was like stepping into a living rainbow, stunning. There is a series of ponds that lead from one to another, with stepping stones. It's about four miles out of Dorchester, very posh – the whole area shrieks of money.

When we entered the old house I remembered coming here for the weekend after we'd scattered Corrine's ashes, when I was fourteen. At last I could see why Vivienne and Amy were called the V&A! The whole place was stuffed full of Victorian antiques, exactly as I'd been told to expect. I thought I'd find it off-putting this time, but once again, I loved it.

It has an Alice in Wonderland feel about it. It's like being inside one of those Victorian dolls' houses – you know, the sort where the front opens off like a door. The rooms here are so perfect, with matching wood in dark oak, corner cupboards, quirky little tables, and mirrors everywhere. It makes me want to be a writer again, just so I could describe it. Maybe one day I will.

On the grass at the back was a marquee, set up with a wooden platform for dancing, and it's this that I really want to tell you about. Well, you know this was a wrinklies' party, mostly over fifties, except for Lotte, and someone called Suzy as the youngest guest apart from me. You might've thought I'd be bored out of my brain, but not a bit of it.

Years and years ago when Corrine (Dee's friend that died) set up the singing group, these two friends, the V&A, were part of it. So I knew they were musical, but I'd never expected they could dance as well. I went along because I liked them and for Dee and Lotte's sake because they had been really looking forward to this 'bit of a do'.

Your mum was something else. Woah did she let her hair down. Well they all did. They had been around in the fifties and sixties and they loved all the golden oldies. Don't laugh. These old women can really move. I have never seen anything like it in my whole life and I tell you, Tracey, forty is no age at all. Vivienne was seventy and she danced all night. Admittedly, Amy didn't, because she has arthritis, so she sat most of them out. But Viv likes to lead, 'be the man', and your mum likes 'to follow'. She was a real goer and I liked her a lot.

The thing is that they were laughing together about the name of a dolmen on Dartmoor called Spinsters' Rock. It's near 'Three Chimneys' – the holiday cottage we are going to tomorrow after all the cleaning up has been done. I'm writing this the morning after the night before, as they say.

Anyway, we started off in the house with pre-party cocktails. I went a bundle on a coconut one with rum in it. The trouble is that they made them as long drinks with little straws in and paper umbrellas, and they tasted harmless. But they were lethal! I was swigging mine like lemonade till Lotte warned me. So when we went out from the warm house into the cooler air my legs buckled under me. The cool air hit me like I'd been punched in the chest. We watched the sun set over the garden, which was wonderful because they lit the garden ponds after twilight with lamps and the reflections twizzled down deep into the water.

Then food appeared – dips and spreads, vol-au-vents, quiches, salads and pasta dishes. Profiteroles, trifles, fruit salads, everything you can think of. Lotte warned me to eat a lot so that the drink wouldn't affect me so badly.

Then all these lumpy old ladies took to the dance floor and turned into something else. They were so graceful, moving with practice and ease, floating, hovering, dipping and gliding. swaying this way and that way to the rhythms. You know how seals are awkward on the land then they slip into the sea and they're in their element, diving and surfacing, with perfect smooth curves? Well, the women were like that. In their element.

They did some traditional ballroom dancing, quickstep and veleta, foxtrot and tango. Then the woman DJ they'd hired from Southampton started on with Elvis and the Beatles and they all began rock and rolling. The coconut and rum was swaying me, more than a little, and I was still a bit dizzy, so I sat it out with Amy just ogling and laughing. I don't know the first thing about rock and roll but I swear your mum's feet never touched the floor.

I was too shy at Mere Cottage to go with Dee and Lotte when they went disco dancing in Brighton or I might've had an inkling of what 'Party night at The Froggery' would be. Now I've got the bug and by the end of the evening I was learning all the steps and swinging along with the oldies. Who'd have thought it? Them teaching me how to have a good time! I loved it and I missed you and wished you were there.

Then they came to Elton John. It was the song called 'Crocodile Rock'. Well, they were well oiled by now and the music was pounding out so they all changed the words to Spi-in-sters' Rock. I laughed until I cried. Amy said the laughing made her arthritis ache but she didn't care, she went on laughing anyway.

They were wearing a colourful assortment of party clothes. Amy had on a long frock, black velvet, very expensive, and she looked really cute, with a flowy sort of scarf pinned around her shoulders. Vivienne wore a more butch outfit of black velvet trousers and an embroidered silk jacket from Hong Kong over a black silk blouse.

Lotte and Dee were both in trousers, and shiny shirts, and they both had dark black jackets, very posh looking. I'd not seen them dressed up before. Then all the others had a variety of dresses and trousers, and one older woman was even wearing a tux. She was really beautiful. She had deep dark eyes and olive skin. She's in the singing group as well, and she's called Ruby.

There were about forty of us altogether. Three of the women had daughters with them and one had a dyke daughter, Suzy, but she was thirty, miles older than us.

Some had been married and some not. While I sat next to Amy she filled me in on who they all were. It was like a lesson in lesbian history.

This morning after I'd had breakfast, I wandered into their library and you have never seen so many lesbian books in your dear sweet life as there are on those shelves. I mean, Lotte has a few, but they seemed to have yards and yards of them. All about women who lived together down through the ages. I liked *The Ladies of Llangollen* best. They ran away from Ireland because they were so in love with one another, and set up home in Llangollen in Wales, and everyone knew they were out. So it seems that spinsters have been rocking around the clock since the time of Sappho, doesn't it? It made me want to take the book and ram it hard down my mum's homophobic throat – except it would spoil the book. Homophobic's not a word that's easy to write after a night on the tiles. I don't use it usually, but I got used to it with Clause 28. I'm learning new things all the time now.

Anyway, I have to go now, to help clear up, and then we leave this afternoon for the holiday cottage and the real Spinsters' Rock. There is a legend attached to it. Tomorrow night there is going to be a candlelit storytelling session with some of the V&A's local friends. They know a woman musician who plays the Celtic harp, so they have invited her along, and someone else who plays guitar. They have promised to tell me the tale of Spinsters' Rock. When the story is being told I will tape record it for you. I can borrow their recorder from here and take it with me. Amy has been working as an astrologer for years and she uses it to record all the details of people's charts for them. She says she is happy to lend it to me, so that you can be part of it. As I said before, they may have more money than you or I will ever see, but they are also very kind. They asked me to send love and strength to you by day and by night until you get out of that place.

Later.

Three Chimneys Cottage
Moretonhampstead
Dartmoor

It's a lovely place and you will find your kestrel here. I know it. I just know it.

I think of you all the time. You look like a very young version of your mum.

I get the impression that she is very sorry about the way she mistrusted you. She knows my story now and I think it shook her up – made her realise she should hang on to what she's got. I hope you can forgive her. It's an amazing thing to have a mum who is willing to say sorry. I wish I had one.

I enclose the tape, and I do hope Sylve will lend you her tape recorder so you can listen to it.

Write to me soon.

I will come and visit you again when we get home, before I go to the clinic.

Your friend,
Gail

Tracey
October, 1988

It's just after Gail's visit. I was so glad to see her, again. I told her how much I had enjoyed her letter and the tape. I am going to send it to Esther, for her research. In two days' time Gail will be under the anaesthetic for the first of her operations. She is brave. I'd be scared stiff of them coming at my head with their knives and scalpels. I hope they know what they're doing.

Things don't change in here but I am changing. I am strong again after a bad time last month. Sylve still takes care of me. She was a bit off about Gail but I told her she was my cousin and it seems okay.

Sally came to see me again and brought photos of Billie – she's so beautiful.

Mum will come again next week. I'm glad. It seems that Esther really did work magic on her. But I think Gail has as well. She talked to my mum at the party, and afterwards. Funny to think that Clause 28 came and went, and in the middle of it all I got all my family back. Up yours, Margaret.

Dear Esther,

Things are improving for me now. This hell hole hasn't changed but I'm coping with it much better. I've got my mum back, thanks to you and Gail, and that helps a lot.

Gail is in the clinic. The operations are very tricky, because her ear is a tight space to cut around in. Please, will you light a few candles for her?

Here is a legend from Dartmoor you will like because it's

your sort of thing. You did all the spinning stuff, didn't you, for *Three Ply Yarn*. You, Dee and Lotte were the three strands of wool. My mum was the hand holding the three strands, right?

So, why don't you do another book, Ess, about all of us? This time, Dee, Lotte and you, Ess, are the three legs of the Spinsters' Rock and you all know Nell, so she is the capstone, like the umbrella, linking you all together, over the top. Besides, that's my mum to a T isn't it. She always did go 'right over the top'! Otherwise you wouldn't have had to tell her off, would you?

Spinsters' Rock is just right to describe you all. I'm no writer like you are, Ess, but I can see pictures in my mind.

I've run out of paper.

Bye for now,
Tracey

THE LEGEND OF SPINSTERS' ROCK

At the beginning of time, and just before breakfast, three women sat spinning on the edge of the continent of Europe. They talked as they span, watched the shadows on the sea, and sometimes they sang. Their words were of hope and the meaning of life. They were the first philosophers.

They discussed the cycles of the moon, the origins of the universe, who should do the ironing, and what they should have for breakfast. They sat and span, and as they handled the thread and twirled their distaffs, watching the rising sun in the north east, they observed the upsurging of the mountains, the plummeting of the valleys, the hanging walls of rock, the shifts and schisms, the splittings and the fracturings. They were witness to it all and still they spun.

It became a rare and and rugged landscape in which they lived and worked. They span a thread for every day, of every year, of the formation of the earth around them. So, they span for eons of time, and still they had not had their breakfast.

114

Four hundred million years seems to us, as mere mortals, a very, very long time ago. And the planet is older still than that. But, about then, give or take a few hundred years, a mere fingerclick to the three who span, they noticed that the crust of the earth began to separate into a dozen or so vast moving plates. And yet they continued to spin.

The earth's crust had started to pull apart. For a million years the vast plates slid away from each other, like lovers after a quarrel, drifting apart, separating, abandoning one another to fate. I do not love you any more. I need my own space. And still the women span.

Yet the pulling apart was not permanent, and the process was reversed. For the next million years the huge plates moved back to touch each other again, sometimes colliding, like lovers who regret the original separation. I need to be close to you. I miss the old intimacy, don't you? And still the women span.

We are the three fates, they sang. We watch and attend. We listen to your splittings and your fusings. We cannot advise you.

Pulling and pushing, pulling and pushing, the surface of the earth shifted this way and that as the continent of Europe was created. Mountains the height of the Himalayas rose from the depths, then crumbled again, fracturing and faulting over sliding foundations. Great holes opened up in the ocean floors and into them rolled the sediments from the mountains that were falling apart, jostling for space, unable to accommodate each other.

Sometimes the mountains resembled lovers in ecstasy, their arching forms sliding against each other, slipping and gliding, heaving and sighing. And still the women span, and sang, and told their stories, and combed their hair in the early morning light.

Elsewhere across the continent of Europe there were giantesses who liked to throw their weight around. As the three women sang, and span, the giantesses were not idle.

They did not spin and neither did they weave. For their task was quite different. They were the great stone gatherers, and had been from the beginning of time.

Around their vast midriffs they tied their enormous aprons, fastening them in double knots, which only they had learned. Imagine their aprons, if you can. For there was every colour of the spectrum and more besides. Colours that we have never seen nor could ever imagine: the hues of the auroras, the blendings of the sun dipping into the ocean. Vibrant and life-giving colours, delicate and dismal colours, frightening and awesome colours, sombre and subtle colours. The colour of marble, the swirl of ocean, the washing of sky and the tints of cloud. The aura of thunder, the shades of lightning, the depths of rivers, and the shadows of the moon.

The giantesses strode and they gathered. They searched for boulders and pebbles, shudderings and fragments, and when their aprons were full they ran, leaping from hill top to hill top as sure footed as gazelles. Shape-shifters, land sculpturers, the mega million tonne women danced from summit to summit with ease and grace, skimming the horizons, searching out sites onto which they could tip the contents of their aprons, slinging boulders down the rivers to the sea.

And still the three spinners handled their thread, and spun their yarns and watched the world being formed and told their tales and waited for their breakfast.

Eventually, amid the turmoil of falling apart, the moving plates again separated, and as they did a strange event began to take place. The earth's crust at the edge of the land mass of Europe had, by now, become so thin that molten rock could thrust upwards and upwards through it. So, the great granite tors of Dartmoor were born.

The appearance of the granite of the West Country was a slow and painful birth, which was noticed by the three spinning women, but they did not cease their work. The Dartmoor granite was first, the oldest child. The granite of Bodmin Moor came next; and was followed by the St Austell region, taking its time and emerging in a different form, as china clay. Last of all came Land's End and West Penwith, like twins, the youngest ones.

The three spinsters of Dartmoor had completed many skeins of thread. They had watched as the mountain chain of Europe had shrunk back into the oceans and faulted and fractured. Only hints of the hundreds of millions of years of turmoil could be seen – parts of France pushed over and tipped down into modern Cornwall, and the arrival of Lundy Island, a tiny granite bump that came from a volcano out in the Atlantic and slid along a fault line to end up off the north Devon coast.

When is early morning at the beginning of time? How old are the three women who sit spinning on the edge of the mid-summer moorland?

They do not have the answer to that question and they do not mind. They were always there, whatever always might mean. Your need and mine to know the details is not of any concern to them. Laughing and enjoying their work, they spin their yarns. We catch a glimpse of them one morning just after dawn.

They are spinning in an open field not far from their dwelling, discussing among themselves where and how to place the stone of a dolmen they have decided to build.

They have gathered so much yarn by now, although now has little significance for those who do not live inside linear time. Too much yarn to weave with, they would be there for ever. So they transform it into rope, by twisting the yarns together. They coil the rope into neat piles around them.

They have in mind to choose three large pieces of granite from the array of boulders lying around on the moor. They are doing this as we watch, this one midsummer morning. They have plenty of time. There is no hurry.

All around them, the land is very peaceful. The granite sparkles in the sunlight with hundreds of thousands of quartz crystals mixed in with mica and feldspar.

Way to the south east the crystal making was different, because the temperature and speed of the cooling process changed the feldspar and created china clay. It's just as well, for the clay makes a smooth and pristine surface on the paper on which I shall write this story down.

I digress. But no matter, for the three spinning women are engrossed in wandering the edges of the moors, selecting their favourite three uprights for their dolmen.

They assess the weight and height, the colour and texture, the shape and the ease of getting their strong and tensile ropes underneath.

They have decided upon the first upright and are satisfied. They return to where they had been spinning amid the piles of rope, shoulder the loops easily and stride to the first granite boulder.

They rope it carefully, leaving six ends. They place some heavy wooden rollers under the open edge and, taking a rope each over their shoulders, they begin to pull.

It takes a little effort but they are strong women, undaunted by the task. Steadily they move the vast granite load, pausing now and then to change the wooden rollers, until they reach the site of their dolmen. They leave the boulder to rest on the rollers, pick up their axes and cleave out a deep socket to take two thirds of the length of the stone. Then they pass the six ropes over an A frame and using it as a pivot, they simply tilt the upright until it slides neatly down into the ground. It is perfect. It looks splendid.

They return for the second stone, roll it and drag it back, cleave a second pit hole, pull the guide ropes over the A frame and tilt the second upright into its socket. It is perfect. It looks splendid.

They return the final time, to collect their third upright, roll and drag it into position, cleave a socket for it, pass the ropes over the A frame, and again tilt the tall granite upright into its prepared socket deep in the ground. Together, the three stones are magnificent.

With the three uprights in position, the women tramp back on to the moors to find a capstone. There are many to choose from but it must be exactly right in size and shape or it will not appear balanced. They use their feet as measurements to pace out the sizes and there it is, the perfect stone. It weighs only sixteen tonnes, no problem. It measures forty-seven feet by ten. They know it will look superb.

They need extra ropes and rollers for this one, and to be honest, it does strain them a little. But it's not an impossible task and they roll and drag it back to the site. They take up their axes and pile up the loose earth that was excavated from the socket pits until it forms a sloping ramp reaching to the full height of the uprights.

They shoulder their ropes again, singing lustily to give themselves courage, and, with the rollers in position, they heave and heave and heave until the capstone moves slowly upwards, tilts over and settles atop the three legs.

Then they take off the ropes and roll them neatly a little way off. They take up their axes and shovel the rest of the earth until it all but covers the whole dolmen, leaving an entrance which faces the midsummer sunrise over the hill to the north east.

When we are old women, they say, and we have gathered around us a tribe of loved ones, of all ages, to live and work with, have fun and make songs with, to drum and dance with, and celebrate the beauty of the earth that has formed itself all around us, then we shall have this dolmen where the ashes of the dead can be laid to rest, and anyone who wants to can come and stay, and talk to its guardians. It will be a place where the living and the dead can tell their stories and know themselves to be wise.

Grass will grow over it and it will be green and domed, and everyone will know that, once, we watched the earth being made here as we sang our songs and spun wonderful yarns and all of it was accomplished before breakfast.

Book 2

Tracey
Spring, 1997

When I was let out of prison, I came here to Mere Cottage. That was in 1990, seven years ago.

The front garden was full of primroses and bulbs. It was March the sixteenth, lunchtime. Lotte and Dee showed me my room, upstairs – a bedroom they planned to use for the B&B, eventually. It was generous of them and I said, 'I'd have to rent somewhere anyway, so why don't I rent off you and go for housing benefit?' So I did and I became their lodger.

I'm fast at mental arithmetic – you have to be down the market – and I didn't want to rip them off. From April to the start of October they could get twelve pounds a night B&B or twenty-four if they did a double. That'd be between £80 and £150 a week if they were full. They'd not always be full, so say two thirds. Call it a hundred a week and call it two thirds full, that's over £2000 for six months. Suppose I brought in forty a week all year. That was about right. So we were all happy and it suited us.

Downstairs again we had soup and bread, then Gail took me out to her place. Gail didn't live in the house. There was a dip in the land, in the huge garden. They'd found the ruins of a summerhouse with an old Victorian tiled floor.

'You kept that quiet – you live in a summerhouse?'

'Wait till you see it. It's not exactly a summerhouse any more. Come on, I'll show you. I wanted it to be a surprise.'

'It is. You're not wrong.'

I followed her down a gravel path, under some old apple trees, and round a corner. Then I stood open-mouthed at the sight of Gail's place.

'Did you build that?'

'All my own work,' she said, proudly.

We ran down the three redbrick steps to a gravel area by the door. I'll start at the top and work down. The roof had a set of ridge tiles, red, with little curves and points. Victorian. You can see them on old terraced houses in London, where yuppies've moved in and done 'em up. The roof tiles were also Victorian red. The summerhouse itself was wooden, with walls on three sides; wood shingles, all cut by hand. The front was made up of Victorian window frames with stained glass at the top but clear underneath. Two of them were hinged so as they'd open outwards.

The door was pine, with stained-glass panels, like the original would've been. The tiny house was divided into two parts – one third was the kitchen and shower, and two thirds was Gail's bedsit, with a wood stove, whose chimney came up through the roof.

'Did they let you rebuild it, just as it was?'

'Dee and Lotte, you mean?'

'No. The council...you know...' I waved my arm in the vague direction of Brighton. 'Them?'

Gail coughed. 'Sort of. I rebuilt it without the inside done. Just a summerhouse with a tiled floor. My uncle got me the roof tiles and the door. I made the rest myself. Then the council bloke came. He was all right. After it was approved it was summer and warm enough to sleep out here. Then Uncle Stuart said, why not put in a shower? He did the plumbing for me, it just runs down a soak-away. Then we built a wood shed out the back and I got a new camping kazi. It goes on the compost.'

'Oh yuk.'

'It's fine. It's not like that. The new ones are for those touring vans. It's at the back of the wood shed. It was a birthday present.'

'You had a bog for your birthday?'

'Yes.' Gail laughed. 'Dee had two tonnes of grit!'

'Whatever turns you on.' I grinned at her. 'It's all lovely. Just lovely.'

'I set to after the Council had been and started on the roof, insulating the inside and making it into a kind of tea cosy. Like those Swedish houses that need hardly any heating. The glass is double-glazed and all we had to do was cut a hole in the roof for my chimney. It takes the pressure off us all indoors and I can invite them out here for a meal, if I want. My little cooker works off a gas bottle and it's just right.'

'How big is this place?'

'Twenty by twelve. We added to the original size.'

'It's the same as the downstairs of my mum's house in Reeve Green.'

'I love it. It's my own place and it gives me some privacy. I've got lots of work now and I don't need much money. I do the maintenance on the house and give Dee a hand with the garden. Fallen on my feet, haven't I?' Gail sighed. 'Then I met you...'

'Is this where you do your writing?' I asked, quickly.

A small, dark, wooden desk had been fitted expertly across a corner. 'Yes, but it's only a hobby. I'm a carpenter – I'm still my uncle's apprentice, officially. Couple more years to go. He wants me to take some exams and do some courses.'

'Will you?'

'Dunno. Never been to school since I was ten. I don't know if I could. I'd have to go *into* a college. You know? Maybe.'

Gail called her summerhouse 'The Cabin'. We stayed there talking all afternoon. A plan was forming in my mind, but I didn't say a word right then.

That night we four had dinner in Dee and Lotte's kitchen, a huge casserole, best food I'd had in ages.

Gail went off to The Cabin; and I went to bed.

I lay in my room, taking it all in, thinking over the events of the day. The room was simple but felt like luxury. A wardrobe and chest of drawers, wallpaper, curtains, and a wide double bed. But I couldn't relax. Pictures came and went. Metal bars, prison doors, keys. Sylve leaning over me, touching me where I craved it. She was still inside. Inside prison; inside me. She'd be taking care of somebody new tonight. I missed her. But I had to move on, without looking back. I had this one chance. No one was going to take it away from me.

A night owl screeched, making me jump. But he was minding his own business, in a distant barn. The wind caught the trees, branches creaking. I couldn't sleep. So I got out of bed and opened the curtains. The moon was up, a half moon, tilted. The garden was dark and shadowy. I could make out the orchard. Its gravel path shone like a white ribbon. Down in the dip, past the orchard, a wink of light came from Gail's cabin. So she couldn't sleep either. What should I do about Gail?

What ifs were spinning round and round in my brain. I wanted to work outside, not cooped up. I was very strong, willing to turn my hand to anything. But in the country... what do they *do* in the country? Work with the land? Work with animals? Dig holes in the road? What did I want now I was free?

I could find a lover and have a good time. Yes, but money was the first thing. They don't let you stay on the dole, not any more. Things was tightening up. Restart programmes. Gawd knows what else. They would soon be at me. Do this, do that. I'd have to stay a step ahead.

I thought back to the market. It was a doddle. And there was perks. Free fruit and veg. And the fiddle. Change madam? Coppers in the apron. No sweat. Half of me mates there was working and signing on. Might be okay in London, wouldn't get away with it here. First things first. I'd got myself a lovely, lovely place and three good friends. They'd stood by me when I was inside and I needed them.

Back in my double bed, up in my room, I said, quietly, into the dark, 'Come to me, kestrel.'

I climbed on the back of the kestrel, snuggled in between the feathers, closed my eyes and slept.

Gail
Spring, 1997

My earliest memory of loving a girl was Jennifer Bradley in my infants' class, so I suppose I've been a dyke since I was six years old. We sat together at a desk for two, held hands in the playground, always picked each other to walk with on the trail to the swimming baths, shared all our sweets money, and told each other secrets. We hated the same teachers and loved the same colours.

Jennie's mum was everything my mum was not. She had six children and said, 'What's another one, you're no trouble, lovie.' Jennie had three brothers and two sisters, all older, and I went to stay there weekends if Mum was working.

'My mum doesn't like me, because I'm a girl,' I told Jennie.

'That's just silly. My mum likes you. She likes you lots. She said so.'

'That's nice. My mum doesn't like children. And she doesn't like fat people. She's frightened of getting fat. So she doesn't eat much. I like coming to your house Jennie, your mum makes big dinners.'

I loved Jennie for three years. I don't know if her mum guessed that I wasn't fed properly at home but she hugged me and fed me well, and I knew I was welcome there. I shared Jennie's pet rabbit, Thumper, and at night in her bed we snuggled up together like two small sparrows in a nest. They were my happiest times when I was small.

I fell in love with Tracey during my prison visits. Just thinking about her made my stomach do somersaults. I wanted her, and I wanted her to want me.

127

I suspected that she didn't feel the same way about me. I don't know why – maybe I picked it up from the way she talked or the way she looked at me. I was only a couple of years younger than her but she was streetwise and worldly and had been out for years.

I couldn't sleep that first night after she came to Mere Cottage. I put on a thick black tracksuit and went outside, standing in the dark, with my navy anorak hood pulled up.

I saw her silhouetted against her window, watching the moon on her first night of freedom, and I longed for her touch. But I couldn't possibly tell her. Maybe she knew already. She was so experienced, what with Maxie and Sylve and all the others. I couldn't match that. No chance. But I could give what the others hadn't. Real love. I just didn't know how to ask.

It was a deep dark night, in Deanne's dream garden. I waited a while then wandered through the orchard to where the gravel path divided. I didn't go towards the house, but took the other branch and made for the vegetable plot. On New Year's Day we had sown onions, and since then new potatoes, in long rows. We had a trench prepared ready for runner beans, and our breakfast bits of melon and grapefruit peel gleamed like slices fallen from the moon.

I looked up at the moon and asked myself, 'What does the future hold for me? Should I take a risk and tell Tracey? Should I risk it? Would she feel trapped and want to leave?'

My mind was all Tracey Tracey Tracey. I walked the full length of the organic plots, then through a rose arch which would be covered in Golden Showers in June, into Dee's herb garden. I would show it to Tracey tomorrow. It was laid out Elizabethan-style, with separate plots and box borders. It radiated around a sundial and smelled fragrant, even at night. I sat on a wooden bench at the far side, glad to be at Mere Cottage, free of my mother, ready for my future. But would it be with Tracey?

Tracey
December, 1997

Looking back to the first summer at Dee and Lotte's place, I was in a real state. Funniest thing was, I stayed in me room a lot. After two years looking at me prison walls, I got scared of the great outdoors. *Me*, who wanted to get out and stay out. I couldn't believe it. There was just too much open land. The South Downs rolled away from the end of the garden like some enormous swelling sea, stretching off towards the horizon. You could go on for ever and ever, just dissolving away into the distance.

I wanted to be outdoors, but I couldn't bear it. I wanted to rest, but I couldn't sleep. I wanted peace, but I felt suffocated by all the silence. It was doing my head in. So I called Mum.

She said, 'Don't try to sleep, Trace. Just rest – it's nearly as good for you. You've had a rough time, give yourself a break. You can sleep in bits. It doesn't have to be all in one go.'

'Just as well. It's freaking me out. It's bloody weird.'

'No need to swear, Tracey. Go wash yer mouth out with soap an' water.'

I laughed. 'You're supposed to be so glad to talk to me, Mum, and you end up giving me an earful!'

'You watch your words, my girl. I'm still your mum and don't you forget it. But I do love you, babe.'

'Yes, Mum, I know you do.'

I couldn't understand what was happening to me. In prison I was strong. In that hell hole. But I didn't feel strong now, just uncertain, wobbly, unsure of myself. I'd thought that once I was free, I'd just get on with it, like I've always done in the past. But this was different. I didn't know what to do with myself, which way to turn.

Trouble was, I couldn't tell Dee or Lotte or Gail. I just kept to myself out of everyone's way. Dunno why. I trusted them but I didn't know how to explain the whirling in my mind, not to anyone. So I kept me distance a bit. Wasn't easy, though. They're quite a huggy lot. I'm not used to that. Too near. Can't cope. My mum wasn't like that at home. So I'd stand like an ironing board, hard, tall, all closed up. I let them hug me but I didn't hug back. I couldn't.

I was in The Cabin with Gail one lunchtime and we was munching away on cheese on toast.

'I don't want to offend you, Trace, but you're not much into hugging, are you? Is there something wrong?'

'No – it's just I don't want to hug anyone, really. Not used to it, I s'pose.'

'That's okay.'

Only it wasn't, you could tell that it wasn't. She went on, 'Only if you don't like it, I'd prefer to know. I thought maybe it was because of *that* place . . . or maybe it's me . . .'

I didn't like where this conversation was leading. I felt dead embarrassed so I just tried to laugh it off: 'It's just that I dunno what I'm doing or where I am. And being in the country is giving me the heebie-jeebies.'

She sounded very sad then. She said, 'Do you want to go back to the city?'

'Yes. No. Don't know. Nothing to go back for. Nowhere to live there.' I laughed again. 'I'm lost in space.'

She smiled. 'Nice to see you laugh, Tracey. Takes some getting used to here, right?'

'Yeah, that . . . and a few other things.'

She was very brave. She knew what I meant. She needed to know where she stood.

'You've been here since March,' she began gently, but her voice was firm and calm. 'It's June now. It'll be the longest day soon. Midsummer's day. But my Midsummer Dream is only a dream,

130

isn't it, Tracey? I've held off asking you this because I knew you needed time to settle in.' She spoke without hesitating, relieved to be asking what she dreaded to ask:

'I want to be your friend. I *am* your friend. I'll always be your friend. But that's all, isn't it?' Her eyes filled and she tried to hide it. But she had to know. She'd waited a long time. I had to set her free. Free to find somebody who could be what she wanted. So she pushed it, and I admired her courage. She asked again, 'Isn't it?'

Big question. Two little words. All your hopes and dreams can come crashing down if you don't get the right reply. But I couldn't lie to Gail. Not after what I'd been through. I didn't know what my future was, but it wasn't being cosy in The Cabin with Gail.

I looked at her, eye to eye. I owed her that. I said it steadily, soft.

'I am your friend, Gail. You mean heaps to me. But you're right, about me and you. I'm sorry. I just can't.'

'You don't love me. I mean, not in that way?'

'I'm sorry, Gail. I am, really.'

She cried then. She couldn't help it. I felt awful. I said, 'Maybe I should go away.'

But she flared, like a firework that had lain in its nice dry box too long, jumping ready to be lit. 'No you don't. You damn well stay here and make it right. You damn well stay and work your bloody socks off to make this place a going concern. Right?'

'Please, Gail, don't be angry.'

'Angry? You haven't seen angry if you think this is me being angry. You led me a right dance. "Make my soul fly." Where does it fly to now, eh? I waited for you. I waited and waited and you needed me. I loved you Tracey and you made me do the asking. You've been pussyfooting around me for twelve whole weeks. I thought you were the wise one, huh? The older one, streetwise. Well, it seems I was wrong, doesn't it? You're just as messed up as the rest of us. Wise? My arse. Get out of this cabin! Go and dig the bloody garden. Do something fucking useful for a change.'

I flipped. 'Look, I'm sorry. I didn't mean to lead you a dance. I didn't, okay? But you fed yourself on dreams. I never, never pretended there was anything more than friendship. All I wanted was to stay alive and get out of that place in one piece. With me body and mind intact. In one piece, right? Twelve weeks. You think that's a long time, do you? Try doing *real* time, Try doing it hour by hour in that hell hole, instead of this poncy cabin. You want me to get out? You bet I fucking will.'

I ran and ran. Borrowed her mountain bike and rode off. Miles into the country; big skies where kestrels fly. I cycled the hell out of me. I cycled for hours. Got myself as far as Cuckmere Haven and then wheeled the bike down over the fields and through the gates, till I met the shingle beach where the waves pull and suck, pull and suck. Like me and Maxie, on each other's bodies.

Her hands on my body, in my body, my mouth on her, her pearl, in its lovely shell. My mouth on her and my face between her legs and the water flowing around me, pull and suck. Wanting her hands in me, on me, on every part of my skin, my shoulders, my inner arms. Fingers playing with fingers, and her tongue moving over my whole body down toward my clit, down, down, both of us wet like the sea. Both of us not waiting; coming together; loving and needing and wanting one another.

The sea pounded in over the shingle beach and I dropped the bike. Shedding my clothes I ran down across the pebbles and into the sea. The sea, soaking me over and over, and me crying and crying for the good days; the days when I had loved Maxie like Gail loved me, and all I got was betrayed.

Esther
Diaries, late December, 1997

I was alone again. Not part of a teeming crowd in a cosmopolitan city, no longer in San Francisco. Instead I was a solitary figure in a wild landscape, in the toe of Britain. From the moors where I now stood, I could see the ocean. I knew that across its vast expanse was the east coast of America, and beyond that were three thousand more miles of solid continent, some of it snowbound, from whence I had travelled.

My luggage was in the attic of someone's house in Penzance. I had decided to approach my destination on foot. I need to earth myself, to touch the land, step by step towards my future.

The Cornish coastroad bus had dropped me at Zennor village, where I'd had lunch in the pub, and then shouldered my minipack with my overnight things, to make my pilgrimage, and to give thanks by touching a dolmen called Zennor quoit.

Leaving the village behind me, I tramped up the steep hill to Eagles' Nest, opposite which a footpath would take me inland towards the heights of Lady Downs. At the start of the path I paused, and, looking along the coastroad to the north, I saw a tiny red car gleaming brightly against the green, grey and blue landscape. It looked like an out of place Christmas decoration.

How different from the city I had left behind. No longer could I hear the sound of trolley buses, horns, cars, vans and delivery lorries. The hills around me were virtually devoid of people and houses and vehicles. The land was still.

As I stood taking it in, I thought of Evelyn Glennie, the percussionist, for whom all music was experienced not as tune or sound but as vibration in specific parts of her body. I wondered how she would feel with this still land beneath her feet. Did her native Scotland resound with such emptiness and silence? How would I come to understand it and learn from it?

I would miss my women's spirituality group, and their resonance with sound and drumming, but I was ready for this solitude. Ready and waiting for this new phase; spinster, independent woman without a man, and now, once again, without a woman lover. Ready as I would ever be.

Far below me lay a Celtic iron-age pattern of old granite field boundaries stretching to the edges of the cliffs where one or two isolated farms and the distant buildings of Hermit's Hut nestled. A grey tarmac ribbon wound down the hill and up the other side on its way to St Ives. The road separated the farmlands from the moors, which stretched forwards to the north and east as far as I could see. Behind me to the west was Eagles' Nest whose garden, Shima, was captured in words and photographs by Susanna Heron, whose mother, Delia had created the place. Her father was the artist Patrick Heron whose stained-glass window illuminates the entrance to the Tate of the West in St Ives.

I had been told an anecdote about him just now in the pub. A few years ago some military planes were using this coast for practice reconnaissance runs. Local people were very angry. The vibrations from the aircraft made the cows abort in the fields and the hens stop laying. Out went Patrick and began throwing stones. The military weren't best pleased. They complained he'd nearly hit one of their planes. He was unrepentant. 'If I can get your plane with a stone from my garden, matey, then you're flying too damn low!'

Chuckling to myself, I shoved my hands deeper in my pockets and started off along the footpath on to the stone-littered moor. The sun was low and thin, silvery, approaching winter solstice. I walked inland for a good few minutes, then turned again, to take in the vast curve of the sea's horizon, a semicircle of intense winter blue, with the merest hint of green. There was a small wind, enough to bite my hands if I took off my gloves, but pleasant for walking in.

The old granite landscape which was to be my new home

changed in appearance with each turn of my path. The metaphor did not escape me. My path would be solitary for the foreseeable future. I had not anticipated that this would happen, but now I welcomed it, and realised that each of its turns would bring me new gifts.

To the north now there rose huge carved granite biscuits piled up in a haphazard way and I thought of the legend of Spinsters' Rock which Tracey had sent to so many years before.

I loved the old legends. The old women, the strong women, the stone women. I imagined the giantesses with their coloured aprons, strewing the moors with the fruits of their labour.

Ahead now were broken buildings, granite again, but younger than the rest of the moor, mere memories of the recent centuries of tin mining. Checking my map, I found the path to the right, and began to walk south.

Despite its age, the moor was a landscape recreating itself after serious gorse fires the previous summer. The flames had leapt so high that the fire fighters had feared they might jump the road and scar the landscape as far as the sea. Rumours in the pub said that a mad local farmer had started it (for he had done it before), but no one could prove it.

Once a gorse fire catches, it travels via the roots underground and pops up further on. The fire appears to have a life of its own, in charge of its own destiny, rebellious against human control, as if to say, 'You dared me to start this, I'll finish when I'm good and ready.'

Earth, air, fire and water, the four elements. I paused awhile and realised I was crying. This was such a lovely place, yet it had been ravaged by fire. The elements had gone out of balance. Too much fire. And in my life with Phoebe too, there had been imbalance. It was right, this separation. We would stay friends, be friends, across time and across continents. She would be working in Africa again. I was here, home. But where was home? I felt alone in this new landscape. I called to the spirits of the four elements to give me strength. Hadn't I sent strength to Tracey, when she'd been in prison? One step at a time. Stay strong. Never give up.

Tears streamed down my face. It was a lot to lose. The touch and intimacy of Phoebe. Would she find Isobel again, after all these years? She didn't know. Finding someone is not just about knowing their geographical location, is it?

They say grief has five stages. I was familiar with Elizabeth Kubler Ross' wise book *On Death and Dying*. Phoebe and I had allowed ourselves time for the death and dying together. At least we had shared the grief, given ourselves that opportunity for knowledge – for sanity, even.

We'd survived the denial stage. Gone through the anger stage. Done the bargaining: been there, done that, got the T-shirt. We'd held each other in the melancholy days when depression sets in and you're descending into what's known as the real grief. And finally, the acceptance. We need to move on.

Ten years is a long time. There were those who didn't think we'd last ten days, let alone ten years. We had loved and loved and loved one another.

We had kissed every inch of each other's skin, compared one another's nipples – colour, shape and size; licked one another's sea salt from the depths of our sea caves; slid like black and white mermaids over one another's bodies; combed one another's hair; nibbled one another's earlobes; explored lips with tongues as if they were tiny clits, until our own real clits had throbbed with want and longing.

We had played with words and shapes, colours and textures, anointing one another with honey and loving juices, woman-made, natural.

All that and it was never done with, the loving and wanting, the mapping and exploring of one another. We had never grown tired of each other sexually. It was confusing and it led us to disbelieve our unmet needs for longer than was good for us. They say some lesbian relationships get lesbian bed death and the sex all stops. Not for us.

But we needed different things from life and work. She yearned for Africa, for her work there. I longed for solitude, until, day and night, the craving for creativity was suffocating me, overwhelming me. But when we decided to separate, I felt it would take me years to learn to live without Phoebe.

★

On either side of my pathway, the earth revealed charcoaled stumps of burnt gorse. But the moor was rebirthing itself, slowly, painstakingly, bud by bud. Every stump and twig had a few inches of baby gorse, green and strong. Clumps of bracken had also begun again, although it might take fifteen years before all the gorse and heather was re-established, and the familiar riot of yellow, purple and summer green would delight the eye for mile upon mile. Would it take me fifteen years to transform my life from the charred remains?

I climbed a stone stile and rested by Zennor quoit, using my new compass to find the distant landmarks of Ding Dong mine and Nine Maidens stone circle. Only the low sound of the wind kept me company, bringing echoes; memories of the voices of the tin miners tramping home after a long shift; and the witches of Trewey hill, incanting.

I did not have a camera with me, but my mind took many photos of the quoit from different angles, showing the three uprights and the fallen capstone. I picnicked in the lee of the quoit, sheltered from the breeze, with contented appreciation of the utter quiet.

In the rest of the country, people would be zooming about, shopping and pacing themselves in the run up to Christmas. The radio told daily of traffic congestion as relatives and friends zigzagged across the country for their annual get-together. But the busy times on the moors were long gone with the closure of the mines, and the only zooming would be done by dragonflies in the summer.

So I sat there listening to the silence, until the sun dipped to the south west, the air began to chill, and I made my way back towards Eagles' Nest and the rough track that would take me home to Hermit's Hut.

Lotte
December, 1997

Our Mum, Rene Clegg, married a Canadian GI, and went with
him to Canada after the war. When things didn't work out for her
there, she came back to Grammaclegg's home, pregnant with me,
and with little Esther toddling along beside her.

In a way, our Essie was following in Mum's footsteps. She didn't
marry a man for love (she had more sense). She married for a
passport and when she flew back she was carrying inside her the
seeds of her first novel. And Hermit's Hut in Cornwall was the
perfect place for her to give birth. Come the first of May, when
all the folks in Cornwall would be jumping over the Beltane fires,
she'd be fertile, looking forward to her first harvest.

'You know, Dee, I think our Essie's going to be okay in this
new place,' I said as we were driving down to meet her on her
first day there. 'I think Mum'll watch over her. She would
understand. She did almost the same journey herself.'

'Hope so, sweetheart. Sounds like Essie really needs the
solitude. She's chosen a beautiful place to get inspiration. These
moors are wonderful.'

'They are too.' I smiled at her and fell silent, enjoying the
scenery.

I thought about dreams and how Esther had always wanted to
be a writer – letters, poems, short stories, diaries, or rather,
'journals' as she was taught to call them in her writing class.
Seemed a bit posh to her, not the sort of word a young lass from
Yorkshire would normally use.

Now she wanted to write a novel – a book about all of us, the
story of our lives in the later years of the 1990s, and how we

138

loved, or lost, then loved again; how we simply kept on going. I thought of Gail, whose dream to be lovers with her best friend had not come true. I loved Gail very much, and to see her so unhappy really tore at my heartstrings.

Esther had sung to us a goddess celebration song about times changing. I wasn't *at all* into that sort of thing, but Esther was now. I could imagine her dancing around a fire, chanting, 'She changes everything She touches, and everything She touches, changes,' like one of the witches of old Zennor. The song was called 'Changing Woman', so it seemed just right for Essie because she had changed so much in her years in America. She said she wanted to search. She learned the word from Mary Daly's *Wickedary*, which was her new dictionary. Research, said Essie, was her old way of finding things out. Now, she wanted to break through all the boundaries and learn in new ways. To search. The local legend was that if a woman went to dance nine times around the Witches' Rock at Zennor, under the full moon, then she was sure to become a witch. As Essie spoke to us, she laughed wickedly. She was full of possibilities for the future.

Anyway, it was through friends of Phoebe's that Esther heard about Hermit's Hut. There'd been this rich woman, donkey's years ago, who'd had the original two-roomed granite house. Her name was Harriet, and she holidayed there to get away from it all, to be a hermit for a while. It had been a single storey stone building with granite walls a foot and a half thick. Well, she'd need them against the wind on the north Cornish coast, wouldn't she? And in Cornwall they always have to put the main door at the back, away from the wind. It comes in fierce, off the sea.

She'd had two wings built on to it to enclose a sunny garden, and when she died, she left it to women as a trust fund for the arts. In her will she said that her lover, Denny Slater, could live there for the rest of her life as a warden, looking after the place and the Hermit's Hut Foundation. That was back in 1989. But Denny was grief-stricken and emigrated to New Zealand, which she called Aotearoa.

So, a group of women ran the trust fund after that. They organised for women artists, writers or musicians to stay for a month or so to work on their own art, and there was no need for a warden. But now the whole place needed refurbishing and someone had to be in residence to see it through.

Esther applied for the position and sent an outline of her project. She told the organisers about Spinsters' Rock and the novel she wanted to write, and, hey presto, she got the tenancy. The wardenship was temporary, advertised as one year to start with. It was rent free because of the inconvenient location. The new tenant would only have to pay for fuel and the phone and such like. It suited our Essie down to the ground.

We drove on, gaining height. Dee seemed very relaxed and happy beside me. The timing of this holiday had suited us both.

Presently, she smiled at me and said, 'We could stop here a minute, if you like. There's a dolmen like Spinsters' Rock in that field.'

So, we parked beside the Cornish hedge at the roadside, and climbed a stone stile to get through to Lanyon quoit. Again, three uprights and a capstone, but this time the capstone was oblong and flat, not like the mushroom shape we'd seen before. Our guide book said this one had been reconstructed. It seemed artificial and to us it felt a bit dead, not a lively, lovable place like Spinsters' Rock. We read the noticeboard and took a couple of photos, then drove on, slightly crestfallen.

But we were excited to be on our way to Esther's, and our spirits soared again as we dropped from the high moors towards the north coast. Joining the St Ives road, we could see the enormous cliffs falling to the sea and the scenery astonished us. Even at this distance we could see the waves as they surged, crested and broke. Near Zennor the coast road was spectacular, dipping and rising, with the sea dazzling far below us and great crags of granite to our right.

We drove up past Eagles' Nest, to the very top of the hill, over the crest then down again. We pulled in beside a small red car parked in a layby and there, between us and the wintry sea, was our first sight of Hermit's Hut.

The grey granite buildings nestled in a fold in the distant cliffs. We got out of the car and stood for a long time, buffeted by the wind, contemplating Esther's new home.

Back in the car, departing from the north coast road, we took a rough farm track which wound towards the sea, occasionally doubling back on itself. It was far from easy going.

'Good thing this is a hired car; wouldn't fancy the suspension on our old banger.'

'Essie'll need a jeep.'

'Well, she warned us it was remote.'

'She wasn't wrong. Where's the chocolate shop, that's what I want to know!'

'And we thought we lived out in the wild.'

'Our place is urban compared to this! Look, here's the gate.'

It was a heavy-duty wooden gate, of modern design, painted deep matt black, and it bore two nameplates. One gave the manufacturers' name, some firm in Truro. The other said simply, *Hermit's Hut*.

I leapt out to open the gate and Dee drove through on to a gravelled enclosure, with a double-fronted barn near by. She parked, climbed out, and we took our bearings.

We were standing on a flat gravelled turning area with two barns separated by a tall granite wall. In this there was another arched gate. It had a slit for a letter box, and was solid, also painted matt black. It fitted so snugly into its arch in the wall that no one could see through and the wind couldn't blow through.

We went through the arched gate, and into the enclosed garden which was about a hundred foot long and seventy foot wide, designed with winding paths, shrubs, climbers on the, walls, and many roses, all in desperate need of some pruning. Here and there daffodils broke the surface of the soil, telling us we were much further south than Mere Cottage.

'This is lovely,' said Dee, as we walked towards a long conservatory that ran the full length of the back of the original two-roomed granite house.

'Yes, but the trust fund isn't wrong about it needing work. It's not as bad as our ruin was, but look at it, Dee – peeling paint, leaky gutters, rotten windows, slipping tiles, wobbly drainpipes.'

'There speaks the voice of experience, Lotte?'

'You can say that again. I'm glad ours is done, aren't you? I love our place but I wouldn't want all that mess over again.'

'Rather Esther than me,' Dee said, as we inspected the cracked panes of glass in the conservatory. We stood a moment inside, looking up at the glass roof, taking stock. Then we came to the solid wall of the original small house. I reached for a huge doorknocker in a heavy wooden door. We heard it reverberating and then the door creaked inwards with a balanced weighted swing and there was my sister, beaming at us.

'Essie, oh Essie, this is wonderful. Well, you've certainly come up smelling of roses!'

'Hello, you.' Over my shoulder, amid big hugs, she said, 'Hello Dee, welcome to my new home. Come in both of you. It's lovely and warm, the Aga's oil-fired, stays on low all the time. I've got the kettle on. Come on, make yourselves at home.'

Nell
January, 1998

My floor dweller's in one hell of a state. There won't be no more driving for my Fred. Not after this. Whatever happens to him now he won't be driving no more. We hoofted out the old car. Went off yesterday to the auction. Not a bad price for it.

Right this minute, right as I'm talking to you, he's in that tunnel up to his neck so's they can scan all his discs again. One after the other. He can still get down the stairs all right. He just can't get back up again. Poor thing. But I'm tired. Weary to my bones with it all. I have to half carry him back up to bed.

Now Ruth next door, she's been in a wheelchair for gawd knows how long on account of her glands. She's gone up to well over twenty stone I think, some fair size anyway, couldn't fit into the armchair. So they puts her in this wheelchair. Then they comes to measure up for her ramp.

We was laughing like drains. Three of them come. How many men does it take to hold a ruler? She only wanted a little slope from her front door to the gate, six feet, maybe seven. 'Oh no,' they says, 'it has to be by the rules 'n' regulations. It has to be curved.'

'Curved?' she says. 'But I don't want it curved 'cos you'd have to pave over me bluebells and I does like me bluebell patch in Maytime.'

'Sorry, madam. Curved. Rules is rules.' So they builds it like the spaghetti junction – this great concrete bypass thing. The garden's only eight foot by thirteen, the width of the house. Now the entire garden is curved concrete. Off to the right, back off to the left, up to the front door. It must be more 'n twenty foot long.

Concrete, with a thick silver handrail. Not a bluebell in sight. Me and my girls we got her a window box and two baskets. Nice.

We could have a bypass like Ruth's if my floor dweller ends up in a wheelchair. I phoned Ess this week and I told her all about it. 'Well,' says Ess, 'maybe you could have a matching pair. Two ramps next door to each other. Hers veers off to the right, yours off to the left. Like a neat set of bookends.' We was laughing down the phone. Concrete city here we come.

He gets his results one week from now and they says fifty fifty. He'll either come out of the hospital walking, or he'll come out in a wheelchair.

He was not in the best frame of mind before this happened. He does try, bless him. After the last time he had his back done, he got himself back on the minicabs, all hours for not a lot of dosh. Then he got depression again and they put him on Prozac.

He was better on Prozac but I couldn't understand him. I tried, but I only know about backs and broken legs and such. When it's his mind I can't see it, I can't see in, I'm just not there, where he is, and I can't help him. It's like a grey cloud lives in the front room. He only smiles for Billie. We niggle at each other like two geese pecking. I don't like it.

He don't like Prozac. It evens everything out and that's better for him, but he says he can't *feel* anything. He can't feel happy and he can't feel sad. It's just a nothing world for him, hour after hour. The Prozac brought him down for nearly a year. He couldn't work. He wanted to, just for something to do, but he couldn't.

But this is different. I can see it. I can feel what pain he is in. I can help him this time.

You know what? We don't get a penny from the social. He gets his sick but the wife is working and not one spare brass farthing have they shoved our way in all that time. And this is a man who used to save lives when he was a fire fighter. You'd think that'd count for something. Bitter? No, I'm not bitter. What good is bitter?

Throughout this time, our Billie has kept Fred going. Without her and her bright little face popping in and out I just don't know where we'd be.

He gets fed up because he can't *do* anything. Like he can't get to the dogs, go to the pictures, off to the horses, out with his mates down the club. He pays a tenner to belong to his club. Then he gets his cut-price beer, so it works out good.

We did think that nice Mr Blair might make a difference to people like Fred. But they're all the same these politicians. He's all for 'working' people. Well, Fred's not exactly a working person is he? He used to be. I'll say that for him. He might have gambled it all away but he did earn it as well, and he was willing.

It's occupational is Fred's back. If you've been a bus driver, or a fire fighter driving the engines, then it's your back that's most likely to go. Sometimes it's the feet and legs. The pressure builds up, from the hard floors and pedals, same position hour after hour, with no walking about or stretching. The buses was worse than the engines in that respect. A real killer for back trouble. Like the farmers in the old days with the old unsprung tractors. It just did their backs in.

I hate to see Fred in so much pain. He's crying with it. To see a grown man cry is not a pretty sight.

I don't know what the outcome'll be, which is why I never left the switchboard. I'm bored with my job but two of the girls that was the most backbiting have gone and things have settled a bit since then. It's not what you work with, is it, what matters? It's who you work with. That's what I think.

But I am tired and the stress and worry about Fred is adding to it. Plus carrying him upstairs every night.

It's not long till I'm sixty-five and then I have to stop. They aren't allowed to keep me on after that. Well, I might've stopped at sixty and I should've really. I'd have liked to start up my own cleaning business but you need capital and nobody I knows has capital. It was a dream, and it got me through a bad patch way back. I heard about this woman who started a cleaning business and she's a millionaire now. But then she had money, and she did the contracts for the big law firms, cleaning posh offices and such like.

I can't get capital and I can't get loans because him indoors is listed on account of his gambling debts. So I might as well stay where I am. Devil you know and all that. They've got a nice little pension fund going and I think Slomners' will treat me right because I've been there so long.

Anyway, what with Fred's bad back and him getting private treatment on my insurance I hadn't better leave until it's all sorted.

So that's me and my life. It's nearly four years now since Christopher. I still got the ruby ring he gave me and the Victorian locket and the sapphire. They were good years and no one can take them away from me.

He said he wanted to leave home. Leave his wife, Carol. We was nine years together, me and Christopher. If Essie had been in London I could've talked and talked to her when it happened. I wrote instead. But letters isn't the same.

He had a son called Derek. The apple of his eye. He didn't want to upset Derek. First it was Derek's GCSEs. Couldn't rock the boat during such important exams.

Carol was the perfect wife. He said it wasn't her fault. She didn't deserve to be hurt. She worked part time at the police station, steady job, nice money. Every November, looking forward to the next summer and a bit of a break in the sunshine, she'd say to him, 'I've got the brochures Christopher, shall I book the holiday again this year?'

He didn't want to go. Told me he was bored with Jersey every year. They always went to the same hotel. Five stars. She didn't have to cook if they went to a hotel. It used to cost him £2000 for two weeks.

Me and him indoors used to take Billie to Margate. Three nights for the price of two. We got tokens from the newspaper.

Then it was Derek's A Levels. He was doing so well. He was a good lad. Couldn't spoil his chances in later life by upsetting him during A Levels.

Me and Christopher sometimes had an awayday. That was if there was a conference on. We'd meet at ten in the morning and travel together. I'd say I was going to see Lotte and Dee in Brighton. Sometimes I did do that. I'd stay a night with them,

146

make it all above board, and then have a night at Christopher's hotel. I liked the intimacy of it.

In the old days me and him indoors used to do it, you know, have a bit. It was all right. But with Christopher I was truly in love. We never had a bit, or did it. We made love.

I tried to tell Ess that it was wonderful – what I said was, 'It was 1001 and porcelain.' I meant it was very important for me, and that it was rare and fragile and beautiful.

Christopher said he really wanted us to set up home together. He had no idea how we lived, me and him indoors: no money; thirteen foot by eleven living room; kitchen you couldn't swing a cat in.

He had to go shopping with Carol on Saturdays. It was a golden rule and he couldn't possibly break it or she would've guessed. Then they'd come home and he'd pick up his kit and go and play football. He trained two nights a week. He led a man's life and Carol fitted round it.

Fred never asked where I went or what I did on Fridays.

Once, Sally asked her dad where I went on Friday nights. 'She goes out,' replied Fred. 'And she comes home.'

So I think Fred knew, but he never asked and I never said.

Then, eventually, I wanted my girls to know. By then, me and Tracey was on speaking terms again. 'Come and meet me,' I said, 'I have something to tell you.' It was after one of Fred's worst gambling bouts. It was in the days when they made the new council tax. The bailiffs had come to the door, wanting to be let in. It turned out that Fred hadn't paid, and hadn't paid the fine neither.

I was so mad. I had bought all that stuff for my little house. *All* of it. Me carpets and curtains, me dark wood desk and matching bookcase, me telly cabinet with the doors that closed. I paid for the frame on that lovely photo of my mum on the wall and the new clock over the fireplace. All of it. And I stood to lose the lot because of him indoors and his gambling.

So I told my girls about Christopher. Well, my Sally took it very well, I'll say that for her.

'You know Mum I always wondered,' she said. 'You go for it Mum.'

But Tracey was visibly shaken. She's her daddy's girl, she is. 'What about me dad?' she asked.

'What about him?' I asked.

'Well, what will he do?'

'Carry on gambling? Carry on wearing a hole in the carpet?'

'Oh, come on, Trace,' said Sally. 'Can you imagine what it's like week in, week out, living with a dead slow or stop. I love him, too, Trace, and he adores my Billie, but he's married to his horses, for heaven's sake! Pull yourself together and get the next round.'

After that it was Derek's university course. He was doing geography and he met a very nice young lady, that's what Christopher called her, name of Rose.

The lovely Rose became the next reason. Mustn't upset Derek while he was doing his last year at uni and then what about the engagement party? Derek must have both his mother and his father there.

I waited nine years for Christopher. I know it sounds like I was a real wimp, but I really loved him.

There was no love indoors. And there was no sex either after the bailiffs knocked on the door. I sent him down to the council offices to sort it. He did, in a way. He agreed in writing to pay so much out of his wages per week, more than he had agreed the last time, and they accepted. He was back on the minicabs by then, so I suppose he thought he could pay.

But I had nearly lost all me possessions over that, paid for from my hard-earned money. Not shared. Oh no. All paid on me tod.

So the next time he turned to me in our bed after the lights was out, I says to him, 'Shop's shut – gone bankrupt.'

In the morning we talked about it. I said, 'Never again try for my body. Don't even think about it. You put my home at risk. Just don't even think about it.'

That was when I needed my Christopher to take me away from it all. To just come and get me, and drive with me into the sunset. He knew I needed him and he said he would leave. But it would be the following summer after Derek's degree.

'What about the engagement party?' I asked

'No,' he said. 'The degree finals are the time. We'll do it. I promise you, Nell. I've never loved Carol the way I love you. I made my promise and I'll be there for you.'

Being there for me. Well now. It was November when the bailiffs called and I had been with Christopher for nine years.

I had to know if he would keep that promise so I made myself wait and didn't sabotage the waiting by being bitter.

I was sweetness and light. I didn't have a go at him. I didn't ask him awkward questions. I bided my time, wrote to Esther in America, and waited.

Christmas came and went that year. A ruby ring from Christopher. The one I still have.

Then, in March, it was just after Mothers' Day and Christopher phoned me at work with two words: 'Carol knows.'

'She what?'

'She says she knows. She says she has known for a long time. Can you meet me at that Pizza Hut we went to last week?'

'I'll be there.' But I realised he wasn't leaving. I had to see him. To hear him say it.

'She says she knows and that she wants me to stay.'

'Are you staying?'

'Just until Derek's finals.' But I knew it was a lie.

'What did you say to her?'

'I asked her if she wanted me to leave.'

'And she said?'

'You aren't going anywhere Christopher. You are staying right here. Okay?'

'So that's it then.'

'I *will* leave, after Derek's finals.'

'I don't think so, Christopher.'

'I promise.'

'All right. I heard you. You've got till the last day of his finals then it's over.'

'Over?'

'You heard.' I walked out of the Pizza Hut without looking back.

The next three months was hell. He phoned me at work and sometimes I met him and we walked round London and had a drink. We didn't go for any meals, not the whole three months. I couldn't eat a thing.

He didn't believe that it would be finished the day of Derek's finals. He was too much of a coward for that.

It took me two years to stop wanting to phone him to find out how he was. The first few months were the worst. And anniversaries. Sometimes on a Friday night I went out with the girls from work; sometimes with Beth and the girls from the estate. I looked in the mirror and there was no light in the back of my eyes. As if someone had simply switched it off.

I decorated all my house and got a new front door. I had Mick in to do me kitchen and Paul the painter to make me a mural in the bathroom. It has a stripy deckchair, with a hat tossed onto the back of it, a straw hat with a blue ribbon, and buckets and spades for Billie. Sand and cliffs and sea.

Little did I know that Essie would come home from America and settle by the sea. Dreams change.

The pain of it has mostly gone now. Faded to a dull ache. I don't envy Carol and her man, trying to stay happy with me as their live-in ghost.

When I asked Christopher how Carol had found out he told me that it went like this. She'd smiled at him, strangely, distantly. She said, 'We women are witches. We *know* things.'

That took me by surprise, that did. That's what I'd have expected Ess to say, her and her women's studies, not Carol. But it's absolutely true. True as I sit here breathing.

Why did I put myself through the final three months? I had to be *sure*. I had to live through every moment of that pain, wanting and hoping, before I could accept that my dreams would not come true.

Otherwise, I would never have really known. I would have lived all the rest of my long life knowing that something might have been if only I had waited. If only. If only. If only is a long, long time.

Yes, I would do it all again, I'd go through every moment of it, and when I am a very old woman, with a purple hat and no teeth, I'll know what the heat of that wanting was like, and I'll have known true loving. No, I don't regret it.

Esther
February, 1998

All over Britain the weather began to deteriorate. At first it was quite exciting. I dressed warmly, bent my head against fairly strong winds and walked the paths and cliffs in every direction from my new home, circling outwards.

I wrote regularly to Laura; and to Phoebe because we were determined that we would stay friends. She didn't want to repeat the losses of her searing break-up with Isobel and I had been through a fire-raising rift with Christine years ago. It had taught me that I never wanted to lose contact with an ex-lover again, if I could help it.

Hermit's Hut
end of January, early February, 1998

Dearest Phoebe,

How are you? How's your new life in Uganda?

I think of you very often, especially as you're in the sun and it's the depths of winter here. It is very dramatic, with high seas and fierce winds, getting stronger each day. I listen now not only to the weather forecast, but to the shipping forecast as well. It brings back the litanies of childhood, because Gramma-clegg always listened to it before the *One O'clock News*: North Uitsere, South Uitsere, Forties, Tyne, Dogger, German Bight.

Thames, Portland, Plymouth, getting closer.

West Finistaire, quite far away over by Ireland.

East Finistaire, getting close now.

Sole and Lundy, that's me.

I have realised that locals don't start counting the force of the wind until it's past force seven. They just say it's a bit of a blow. Force eight and you can't stand up outside!

This is a small granite house with some extensions and outbuildings on the roughest, wettest, windiest, most rugged part of the toe sticking out into the Atlantic. Wrong, it's the Irish Sea. The Atlantic begins after Cape Cornwall, the only cape in Britain.

The gales have started and we are in the middle of them as I write. First to go was the electricity. Luckily the phone line did not come down. The Aga is wonderful and I can stay warm and do my cooking. I have made up a bed in the corner of the living room, and I'm amused at myself for wanting to be a hermit without really having a clue as to what it might mean in this place.

Next to go was the guttering on the south west side. My battery radio picked up the news that this was an unusual combination of force and direction of wind. Just as the guy finished speaking, my radio and TV aerials went hurtling off to St Ives. The wings of the house are tough and tall enough to prevent eddies and turbulence in the garden. Something to do with the proportion of the length to the height – so Harriet who designed the place knew what she was doing.

Two nights ago the rooftiles began to flickflack like a game of dominoes. Click click click. That was only force eight.

Force nine sped up the game and force ten took the tiles away. Luckily, the roof underneath had been previously reinforced and it held firm.

All day Sunday I watched billowing seas rising. Enormous waves swelling, cresting, then cascading as they peak and break along their length in a turbulent boiling of white foam.

These waves hurl themselves at the cliffs with untold ferocity. The sea is bullying, insisting – find me a way through, or I will teach you a lesson you'll never forget.

But these cliffs are solid, formed from the furious outpourings of the Earth Mother's rage. They will not be told what to do. They stand against the unremitting fury of the storm as if they are an army of stone amazons faced with a troupe of frothy ballerinas.

All day long the amazons and ballerinas engage in a push–pull dialectic. I am privileged to be here, witnessing this at such close quarters. My windows are reinforced and I can watch in safety. It feels so intimate that I almost seem to be intruding on some private war.

I am reminded of you and me on our worst days. We have never yelled for days nor thrown things about and we were never deliberately enraged or unkind, but this intensity reminds me of you and me, my dear. Though who was the ballerina and who was the amazon I really wouldn't like to say!

How are you now?

I am really doing okay and I do love the solitude here. Laura has written, asking me to visit her, but at the moment I am writing like crazy for the new book that myself, Lotte and Dee will create, of our lives and our relationship with Nell. Not forgetting the next generation, either. I am working very hard indeed, even when I can't use the computer. Thankfully I was warned about the power failures on this coast and I brought my new state of the art manual typewriter, just in case.

I feel we have been very lucky, you and I; that we scaled the heights and had a long chance to admire the view. We both knew we needed to change and I am so glad we had the time, I should say *made* the time, to make the transition steadily. Not that all my days here are easy without you, by no means. My poor old teddy bear hot-water bottle gets a serious squeezing every so often I can tell you.

I'll stop a while as I want to reread your latest letter.

Goodnight, Phoebe, dearest.

Sweet dreams.

Diary

I was rather tearful when I put down my fountain pen, just now. I always write longhand to Phoebe, for it seems more personal.

Anyway, my best words for her always come out of that particular pen.

I've had mega groceries delivered as I still don't have a car. A jeep is really what I need, but not possible financially. I have extra stocks of coal, paraffin for the emergency lamps, candles and matches, and a gas bottle for the camping cooker that is in one of the barns.

So I am all set up for a long haul if needs be.

I wake every morning joyful to be in my own space. Despite missing Phoebe I do not mourn the endless negotiations that being in a relationship seems to entail. I don't want any relationship for the foreseeable future. I have heard that there is a drumming group locally. That doesn't surprise me, because although this is the late 1990s, Cornwall is always ten to fifteen years behind everyone else. I may go along when the weather improves if I feel the need for the company of other women by then. But I doubt that it will be soon – both the weather and my mood seem set for the time being.

From Uganda at New Year, Phoebe had written to me.

... and I also think of you, while I am up to my eyes in people and you are hermitting there on the edge of the world.

There are amazing things happening here. People remember the atrocities, but are in the process of reconstruction. They are working very hard towards a safe future for this country. In the north there are still rebels who raid the villages; and there are still reports coming in of children abducted and made to fight. Some of the children have witnessed terrible things and will be scarred for years to come, mentally as well as physically. Some of the girls have been sold to older men. But there is optimism here and the hope is that peace will last long enough to give the Museveni government a real chance of making a difference.

My friends have made me very welcome. It was a good decision, the right choice for me at this stage of my research and at this time in my working life. I live as frugally as I can but am in a palace compared to the real poverty in some areas here. It troubles me, because the imbalances are obvious. The main thing that Museveni wants to create is a nation which overcomes tribal divisions, without losing tribal values. I'm working very diligently on the health project - the hours are long, and managing on the meagre funding is like rolling the mythical stone uphill, but I know what I am doing here is purposeful.

I will write more next time. Do send my love to Laura – tell her I'll write soon. And by the way, yes, I would like to listen to the radio tapes of the interviews with Ugandan people. Look forward to getting them. Thanks. By comparison to yours my life is 100 per cent social. I think I've become a people junkie. Take care, dearest hermit.

Your loving friend,
Phoebe

Diary

The rain continues lashing against these windows like a water jet. I thank the Goddess they are storm-proof glass! It is night outside and I have left open the curtains so that the candlelight reflects in the dark obsidian glass.

I think of my spirituality group back in San Francisco. We are approaching Imbolc, the eve of 1st February. It is Bridget's festival, a time of hope when the maiden re-emerges from her Cailleach phase of deepest winter. She arrives, the Spring Goddess, in youthful form, bringing poetry and inspiration. I need her this year. She understands solitude and creative awareness.

I must go to sleep now, but before I do so, I bless this house and give thanks for it, for my safety and my inner calm.

I call upon the spirits of the west, powers of water, to inspire me, to flow with my words here on to these plain white pages.

I call upon the spirits of the north, powers of the earth, sustain this granite house, stone home on stone cliffs, and keep me aware and strong.

I call upon the spirits of the east, powers of air, fill me with your lightness, energy, and gladness. Take my thoughts across the wind, fly them through time and space to my friend for her new life and work.

I call upon the spirits of the south, powers of sunshine, bring me the compassion of your fire, bring me warmth in my heart and in my hearth, on my part of the earth, this winter's night.

Tracey
Summer, 1998

I had run into the sea.

I had run into the sea intending to get wet. I had just felt like dunking myself in the water. That's all. To be there. There in that water.

I stood in the sea, crying. I didn't want to hurt Gail. I didn't *mean* to hurt Gail. I was crying loudly, louder than the noise of the sea. Howling like a seabird in a storm. I didn't know how to trust anyone. I couldn't open up to these new people. Them at Mere Cottage. But I'm not stupid. If I couldn't trust Gail, Lotte and Dee, who could I trust?

A wave pushed at me. Took me by surprise. Off balance. Knocked me over, on to my knees. The shingle was pulling, pulling me down. I hadn't been ready for the power of the sea. Another wave caught me. I was gasping now. It was dangerous, very dangerous. I didn't expect it to be so strong. I didn't want to drown. I hadn't meant to drown. Only dunk myself. I was frightened now. Had it all been for this? To end it all on a lonely beach? After what I'd been through. I heard Esther's voice. Go for it Tracey. You can do it.

I don't know where the strength came from, but I stood up. I lifted my knees, my feet, and started to run. I ran as far forward up that beach as I could. But the shingle slipping under me wouldn't let me. I lifted my feet again, against the water, pulling me back. Then I ran again. Another wave at my knees. Sliding back. The shingle slipping under me. I fought against it. I fought hard. I ran again. My legs up high, my knees as high as I could. I slipped and struggled, but I kept on fighting forwards. I threw myself up the shingle. I heaved myself forwards. I didn't want to be drowned. I didn't want the sea to swallow me. I ran, and ran until I was out of the sea, away from the pull of it.

I was gagging and coughing. Spewing water. Choking and gasping. Huge breaths that wouldn't stop. I crawled on my hands and knees till I reached Gail's bike where I'd left my jeans, shirt and boots. There wasn't a soul in sight. Shivering now. Tore off my pants and T-shirt and wrung them out. Used them to wipe me. Danced about to try and get dry.

I lay a while on me back, shaken and relieved.

I was getting cold now so I pulled on me shirt, jeans and boots.

Then I just sat and stared at the waves thinking. No one and nothing is going to cage me up again. Not the buildings, not the people, not the water. I am going forward. Nothing is going to stop me again.

I will make that B&B a going concern. But I'm not doing it for Gail or Dee or Lotte. I'm doing it for me. I'll stay a couple of summers until it's up and running and then I'm off. Me, myself, I. I am going to learn something new. I've got a plot to dig. Organic. That's the new market. I'll grow my own stuff and I'll have a stall. My stall. No bloke to rip me off. No one to be responsible to but me.

I'm going home now. I'm going to show 'em all. On yer bike Tracey Winters, you got a market business to get off the ground.

I stood up, stretched out my arms. As high as I could, as far as I could. Like a great seabird with wings. I would never be afraid of the sky again. I would never be afraid of the sea or the land again. I was going forward, free as a bird.

When I got home there was food waiting for me in the house, and Gail was red-eyed.

She looked at me warily.

'I'm sorry,' I said.

'I'm sorry,' she said.

★

Well, it took us two full years to get my market stall organised. By then I was growing herbs as well as organic veggies and word was getting around. I read whatever I could and had my nose in a herb book all the first winter.

Then one day I was over at The Cabin with Gail and I said to her, 'Come on, you have to get yourself to that college one evening a week. I'll come with you, wait for you and come home with you, okay? You need a friend. I'm your friend.'

I got her to the college, through the door and into classes. I'd drop her off, wave cheerio, then make for the library. I read all the herb books I could lay my hands on. It was good for me. I'm not the college sort. I still like the outdoors best. But somebody had to get Gail out into the big bad world.

Then the next summer came. I knew I was ready to find a lover and she had to be a dancing dyke. So I started clubbing. No good meeting a dancing dyke anywhere else. I wanted somebody that could dance her heart out, with me or without me.

I sat it out now and then, by the bar, just watching the women dancing. You have to be a bit careful. You can't ask anybody that's with anybody. Oh no. But it didn't take long. That's how I met Jane.

Somebody told me that woman there's into herbs and stuff. So I watched her dancing. She could boogie all right. I liked the look of her the first time I saw her and I thought, yeah, she'll do. She'll do just fine. I sent her cards and bought her flowers. Didn't take long.

I went clubbing a lot with Jane after that. Worked the plots in the days and did my market stall.

'Don't know how you do it,' said Lotte.

'Where do you get all that energy?' asked Dee.

'Saved it up while I was inside,' I said to them both. 'Nothing is going to stop me now. I'll build up my business here, help you get the B&B off the ground, and then, when Dee retires, I'll find my own place and you can have my room for visitors.'

I sort of danced into love with Jane. It wasn't love at first sight. Love takes a long time for someone like me, after someone like Maxie. I told Jane everything, from the start, and she was quiet and kind. She's a medical herbalist and works in Brighton. Eventually we got our own place, with a room for Jane's work.

Been together quite a while now. She's still the best dancer I've ever set my eyes on.

I've got vision again now. I've got what I want. I told Esther when I phoned her. She was in Hermit's Hut by then. I also sorted things out with Gail, though it took some time. She's a good friend now and I'll not abandon her because she stood by me all through Holloway and that is a very big thing in my life.

I like to get things going, so that makes me very like my mum. I get it from her. That's why I used to wind her up. Me and Mum are too much alike, I think.

I know that my mum's dreams have not come true. Not any of them. She's had a hard time. She's not unhappy but she needs real love, like we all do. I think she's a bit passionate underneath all that telephone work and routine. She fell in love and she got betrayed. First by me dad who abandoned her for the geegees, then by Christopher who wouldn't leave his cushy set-up. I know what it's like to be betrayed. But I don't say this sort of thing to Mum. She looks all right again now. The light has come back in her eyes. Mum goes forward with her life, she always has, and I think it's great, to be like that.

It's the network of women friends that keeps my mum going now – them and Billie. With or without me dad, that is the way she would have it, that is how she would live. She phones them all the time.

She and me dad have come to some sort of arrangement. They've made peace, that's it. Peace in their back yard. It's cost them a very high price, but they have settled for it; a peaceful coexistence, where Dad still lives on the floor and Mum steps over him and round him and gets on with her own life.

We were all worried about me dad. Trouble is that Billie will grow up and maybe she'll go away. Whereas Mum will still have all her friends, Dad'll have nothing. He knows that and it takes the stuffing out of him.

He had high hopes originally. He was a grammar-school boy, very good at maths. That's where I get it from. Mum told me that his mum said she was a 'loudmouth low-down brassy bit from Rotherhithe' and would pull him down. But she didn't. He lowered himself to the bottom of his own rope when he got the gambling bug. He knows that.

He got through the back problems but they diagnosed him with clinical depression soon after. I don't know what's worse. He hasn't really got anything going for him any more. He gambled it all away, and he still does. I love me dad and if all dads was as gentle as him the world'd be a different place. But he isn't what me mum needs. I got what I want. I just wish me mum had.

I didn't want me dad left on his own if she went off into the sunset with her Christopher, and I was gutted for me dad, in a way. But he made his own floor and now he has to lie on it.

Once I said to Mum, 'Why is me dad such a doormat?'

She says, 'Now then Tracey, if you don't want to be a doormat, then you don't go round lying on the floor, do you?'

'No, I suppose not. I'm no doormat now to anybody, Mum.'

'That's good. You'll be all right now then, Trace?'

'Yes, Mum. I'm no doormat. Me? I'm going to fly. I'm going to be a magic carpet.'

Gail
Summer, 1998

When Tracey turned me down I was gutted. It took me a long time just to be able to look her in the eye again. I felt guilty about blaming her for not loving me because, all along, I'd known. Really, if I looked deep down inside myself, I'd always known she didn't feel the same way about me. All the clues had been there, but I didn't want to see them.

But after a while it became easier and Tracey made a huge effort to keep the friendship going. In fact, it was Tracey who got me into college. Don't know if I could have even made it as far as the front door without her. I'd sit in that class shaking. Design and technology. But the students were my age or older and it wasn't like school at all. There were two other young women and the rest were blokes. I told them I had a boyfriend and after that they left me alone. I couldn't have come out because I was still much too shy. I could barely cope with college and courses, let alone coming out.

Then, in the summer of 1992, Dee retired and Tracey moved in with Jane. She came five days a week to work on the market garden, but we didn't see her at weekends. I missed her so much after she moved out. I was twenty-two years old and I still hadn't kissed a woman lover.

I eventually confided in Lotte. 'I'm twenty-two and I still haven't found anybody. Talk about a late developer!'

'You don't know when it's going to be the right time, or the right person, Gail. Try not to think about it too much, love. Just get on with your own life, develop your own interests, and then there will be someone there for you.'

'Will there really be?'

'I believe so,' said Lotte. 'I think there is someone walking towards you, but your paths haven't quite crossed yet. But they will, probably when you are least expecting it. Love does not come just how and when we want it. Quite the opposite.'

'How can you know that?'

'I just feel it very strongly. I know that you're lonely and you want someone special, and I believe you will find someone.'

Then she said that she and Dee had been talking about the B&B and had an idea to run by me. They suggested that in the autumn and winter months when we were not very busy, I might try running some woodwork courses. Dee would cook for the women and we could put a couple of extra workbenches in the workshop. Stuart would help me sort it out. I could get six women in there plus me as tutor.

'Just think of it as enjoying working with wood,' said Lotte. 'Not like teaching, if that's a bit frightening. Just focus on the women and the wood.' I had never thought of such a thing, but the more that Lotte said, the more I thought I might give it a try.

'We'd have to make it quite cheap,' I said, adding, 'Some women are on the dole, so they couldn't afford B&B rates.'

'We can do reduced winter rates. Then at least the rooms aren't standing empty. We have to cover hot water, heating and food, and Dee doesn't want to work for nothing, neither would you. But it would be a new interest for you, get you to meet some new women.'

That was six years ago and our woodworking and woodcarving courses for women are quite a thing now.

I love it. At first, I didn't think I could teach anybody anything but I remembered how Stuart had taught me. You break down the skills into small parts and then help the women put each part together in the best sequence. I'd had a brilliant teacher myself, so I had a head start!

Sara came on a weekend course from Brighton. She was my best student the second winter. She is a black woman, two years older than me. Her father was from Cardiff, her mother from

Bristol. They are both black too. She was the first person in her family to go to university. She had finished her degree and was doing her PGCE when she came on the first course. She couldn't have afforded it and we'd never have met, if we'd run the courses at top-whack financially.

She came on three courses – October, November, December – then she asked me out. I went to her place for the evening. It was just before the winter solstice and she would be going home to Cardiff the next day. We were in the house she rented with a friend. They had a real fire, and her friend was out. We were in the living room, just standing by the CD player. We'd been choosing our favourites. She put her hands to my face and leaned towards me. Instinctively I closed my eyes.

She wasn't wearing any perfume but she had some soft coconut wax on her hair. Her lips were full and warm. I opened my lips slightly and leaned into the kiss. There wasn't a sound. It never stopped. It was there, her moist mouth on mine. My arms went round her, and her tongue gently parted my lips. My tongue reached instinctively for hers and the tips just touched. I opened my mouth wide now so that the kiss wouldn't stop, and pressed my hands so gently into her back to keep her there. We moved sideways, without stopping the kiss, to the settee and held each other close. It went on and on until I opened my eyes and then I knew what I wanted to know, and felt that we might never stop kissing.

When we finally paused, she laughed softly and said to me, 'Let me play you the song from Sweet Honey in the Rock. It's called "The Seven Day Kiss".'

'I'm sure I could kiss you without stopping for more than seven days,' I whispered.

Sara was two years older than me, about the same age as Tracey. At first, I didn't realise how significant her age was in the whole scheme of things.

'I have never kissed a woman before. Have you, Gail?'

I shook my head, shyly.

'I've been falling for you. I know how I feel. I'm not playing about, really I'm not. I wouldn't. I'm not like that.'

'Neither am I.'

She nodded and smiled. We were snuggled up on the settee. Then she looked very thoughtful.

I asked her, 'Is there something wrong?'

'No, but there is a lot to tell you.'

Her tone alarmed me a bit, so I asked, 'Have you got somebody else?' She shook her head. 'What is it?'

She took a deep breath, then began to tell me her story.

'I was old going to university, old in my year. I was already nineteen when I started. I did my first year and got pregnant at a party. Gail, I have a daughter.'

'A daughter?'

'Yes. Alicia. She is beautiful. I miss her while I am studying. I had to defer my course because I got pregnant just before I was twenty. I wanted to have my baby and I wouldn't have her adopted. I was going to give up my university courses completely, but my parents put me under great pressure to continue. I'm the first in the family to get a degree. My grandmother is still quite young and lives with us. She is looking after Alicia for me, until I get my PGCE and am settled in a job.'

I thought, 'Oh my God, she is leaving me. I only just kissed her and she's telling me she's going. She'll go back to Cardiff and teach there when she is finished next summer.'

I swallowed hard and looked at the fire. All my dreams were gone up in smoke. 'I've only just met you, and you'll be going. Back to Cardiff.'

She shook her head, smiled very gently, and reached for my hand. I was trembling.

'You are a really lovely woman, Gail. I've been falling for you since the first course. I only meant to do two of them. I'm going to be a junior school teacher and I knew they would be useful. I know they will be. So creative. I told myself I was silly and this couldn't work, but I came on the third one because of you, to see how I really felt.'

'What are you saying?'

'I'm not going back to Cardiff next summer.'

'Not going back?'

'That's right. I want to live and work in Brighton. I need some independence from my family. They have been wonderful, but they wouldn't understand what I need right now.'

'But you've got a little girl. You can't leave her. *My* mum wanted to throw me away. I couldn't bear to think of you doing that.'

'No, I'd never do that. I'm going to work here. Alicia will be school age. The school where I am doing my teaching practice wants me to apply for a job that's coming up in the summer. It's a year's post, covering maternity leave. I'm going to bring Alicia to Brighton. There are other black children here. Besides I have to go through my own coming out process. I cannot do that in Cardiff, *and* deal with Alicia, *and* come out to my family, *and* start a new job. I know this school and I'm happy there. I've also found a very good school for Alicia near our new home.'

'This is so much to take in. I wish you weren't going home tomorrow. A daughter. I never dreamed you had a child. A school age child.'

'I'm sorry this is a shock, but the kiss just happened before the story, probably the wrong way round. But I'm glad we kissed each other. I'm so glad we did.'

'So am I.'

'I know this timing isn't the best. But I wouldn't lie to you. I was very surprised with myself when my feelings started to grow for you, but they were my happiest times recently, there at Mere Cottage. When I heard about Dee's daughter, Isobel, and how you all are around race issues, it freed something up, and the feelings just grew.'

I nodded, but said, 'I need time to think.'

'I know how I feel, Gail. If this isn't what you want, I'll be very sad. But I don't want you to feel under any pressure – it won't make any difference to my plans. I am already in the process of coming out. I have a child. It won't be simple. None of it ever is. But I haven't had sex with men since I got pregnant with Alicia. It wasn't even a relationship. It was just a fling at a party. The father doesn't even know.'

'Was he black?'

166

'Yes. Alicia is a black child. I don't even know where her father is. I left the course and he didn't. We were young and I made a mistake. It happens.'

'It must have been unprotected sex?'

'Don't worry. You're quite safe. I've had tests and everything.'

'Okay. Thanks. Can we sleep together tonight?'

'You sure?'

'Whatever happens or doesn't, I need to curl up with you. I don't want to sleep alone after all this.'

'Good, then we won't.'

We went to bed not long after that and became each other's first woman lover.

I will never forget that night as long as I live. I lay there replete with our lovemaking, thinking, whatever happens to me in the future, there is no going back on how my body responded to that kiss. I wanted her, and I still do. I have to be strong enough. I have so much love to give. If I don't take this chance *now*, then I may regret it for the rest of my life. If Sara is brave enough to risk her family's wrath after everything they have done to help her, can I be brave enough to live out what I'm feeling inside?

The giving and receiving of love is where my dreams are at now. I still don't know all that much about politics, compared with a woman like Esther, who seems to live and breathe politics and spirituality, if her visits, phone calls and writings are anything to go by. But my life is fascinating. Richer and fuller than I might ever have dreamed of. Something made me strong enough to take the chance of love when it came, so unexpectedly. And it was worth it.

Of course, it wasn't easy to begin with, being lovers with Sara, because the little girl who had come to Brighton to live with her mummy, had been torn away from her great-grandma who had brought her up. But, for the first two years, Sara went back with Alicia every half term and long holiday. We were separated, therefore, for several weeks at a time, but we came through it.

I think it was my early childhood of not being loved and

feeling dislocated that helped me be there for Alicia. She had children to play with in her new home, Marcey and Michael, and that must've helped her a good deal. Sara had moved in with another black single parent and they were able to provide each other with mutual support. Then, at the weekends, we welcomed all three children to Mere Cottage.

We made hutches with long runs and gave each child a rabbit and a guinea pig. It took me back to the days of happiness with Jennifer Bradley and her pet rabbit, Thumper. I bought tiny tools for the children, just as Stuart had done for me, and taught them everything I could in the workshop, so that they always had something to do. Lotte was very computer literate, so she set up the computer in one of the downstairs rooms, with lots of games so that their mothers had some free time.

Sara introduced me to a school for deaf and partially hearing children. After my first visit I chose to work there two mornings a week, which taught me more than I think it taught them. My own hearing will never be perfect and it has left me with an inability to travel by air and the possibility of tinnitus when I reach my middle years. So I understand a little about disability and hearing impairment.

I wake up every morning and know that I am happy. Tracey and I are still best of friends and quite often we all go walking together — me and Sara, Tracey and Jane, Dee and Lotte. I am thoroughly loved in a way that I wouldn't have imagined when I was small. It's been a long journey for me, from my panic attacks outside school to this new-found security. But I know where I belong now. It's here, with my family.

Lotte
July, 1998

I have been lovers with Dee now for many a long year. Our life has become a richly woven tapestry, with circles of friends and family. We have chosen the threads ourselves and taken great care over the patterns.

You'd never know we lived just half an hour from Brighton. It is so quiet at Mere Cottage that Nell, who comes now and again to stay with us, detests the stillness. She makes us laugh. In the garden she wears her Walkman, 'to drown out the peacefulness'. There's not enough street lighting for her, and too much open space. She lies awake half the night listening to the floorboards creaking in the dark.

But we love it here. A place like Mere Cottage was what Dee had always longed for, and even if she'd had only me to help her, we'd have tried to do it. By ourselves, we might not have had the time, or the guts, or the energy to sort it out. But then reinforcements turned up in the form of Gail. Three of us. Triple whammy of the very best kind.

Gail is young and strong, and, above all, she is willing. Her arrival brought family life, the gift of love and laughter, and practical support too. From dereliction the house has emerged, shaking off its dust. It reminds me of the house in *Great Expectations* by Charles Dickens. You know, when Estella and the old woman are there in that enormous place and you can't see the corners for cobwebs. Inside our house, even now, we still have our fair share of cobwebbing spiders.

'Well they only want to live and love like everyone else,' says Dee, 'so we don't hassle them.'

They spin and weave like us. But not all our friends see it this way. Especially Nell. Nell can't abide spiders. Indoors or out. Never mind the spinning and weaving. What about all those legs?

Esther tried for years to rid Nell of her spiderphobia.

'Look Nell,' says Ess, 'It's legendary. Spiders are the thirteenth sign. They represent women, and creativity, and hope and work.'

'Yeah,' says Nell, 'I knows all that from books. You've got tomes on spiders, Ess. And they still got eight legs and *I don't like* 'em, all right?'

'It's psychological,' says Ess. 'You've been socialised into fear of spiders.'

'That's right,' says Nell. 'I heard you, Ess. It's all a patriarchal plot. And I tells yer, Ess, you could be the Great Spider Goddess herself, wiv a crown and all, but if you got eight legs and yer moving fast round my skirtin' board, I'm *going to swipe* yer, all right?'

Dee, Esther and myself are spinsters. We're proud of being independent women, women without a man. We are spinning women – we have tales to tell and threads to weave. In Mary Daly's *Wickedary*, she talks about women who weave threads of friendship and trust. She calls those women 'websters'.

Nell is a webster, a woman who brings abundance, good at communicating with us, weaving an intricate web of friendship between us. Her life's so closely interwoven with ours that we can't imagine being without her. She has stayed married to her floor dweller, so she isn't a spinster, which means that our lives are completely different. But we would never think of excluding her.

Nell's other web is her work web. Nell enjoys being competent with new technology and she's always worked. She's been at Slomners' for so many years that she earns a good living and can keep herself safe.

Safety is a key word for Nell. She says that her safe rock is her life tenancy of a council house in London. It is the bricks of her home, the city pavement under her feet as she walks to the station to get her train to work. It is the safe train track with well-maintained carriages that carry her to and from the city. She says it is up to the government to keep that train track safe; to make sure the city is a secure place for her to dream in.

Whenever I think about working lives, I think of women like Esther, Nell, Dee and myself.

Dee and I have always worked. Spinsters like us can be found working as hotel receptionists and legal secretaries, in market gardens and on the buses, in supermarkets and on post office counters, as plumbers and electricians, painters and decorators. We are clerks in building societies and we deliver the post to your door.

We do know some women who don't have to work, and we've been close friends for years with the V&A, whose lovely home at The Froggery has been a happy place to visit.

However, we had a hilarious time trying to make friends with two other wealthy women who live locally. It's a strange story, but was very significant at the time, because we learned so much about who we really were, and what we wanted, by meeting those spinsters from another world.

The Old Hall was a mile or so down the lane from us and was a beautiful mellow brick house with gables and fancy chimneys. The driveway led in over a moat with an old wooden bridge. The Hall's inhabitants, Dorothy and Davinia, were the *grandes dames* of the Horticultural Society, and one evening, which happened to be in the run-up to the elections, we were invited round for dinner.

Dee had joined the society because she wanted to build up our 'local web'. It made us feel that we belonged to the place, that we were a part of things. Anyway, it was going along fine until the cheese and biscuits. I mean, you can talk about almost anything in this country, can't you, but *some* things are still taboo. Well, we'd been through an assortment of niceties – healing, art, theatres, home-made wine, holidays, computers, modems and astrology. Then up comes the question of the election. Davinia asked Dee if she was interested in helping with canvassing.

There was a bit of a hush.

I coughed. I thought, 'Oops a daisy. What now?'

Then Dee, quite gently, it seemed to me, asked, 'For which party?'

'The Conservatives?'

I coughed again. Tried to kick Dee under the table.

But she was braver than I was. She said, quite politely, 'I'm afraid not. You see, we both come from quite poor backgrounds, and we've both always voted Labour. Well, it'll be New Labour now, but that's where we're at, isn't it, Lotte?'

My voice was only about six inches high. I just didn't want this conversation. It came under the title of Not A Good Topic. When I was married, James and Essie would slog it out over politics almost every time they met. Essie would say angrily. 'It's all hushed up! Class always is in this country.' James would attack, and off they'd go for another ten rounds.

So, as quietly as possible and trying to keep the lid on it, I said, 'Yes, we don't want to offend you, I mean it's been a lovely evening, but it doesn't do for people to assume anything about us, really.'

'No, that's right,' said Dee. 'We're from the working classes. We both are. I know some of them do vote Conservative, but not our families.'

'Oh, I see,' said Dorothy, 'I see.'

That was the end of that.

They whistled us through the coffee and into our coats before you could say John Prescott.

On the way home we laughed our socks off.

'I'm amazed at you, Dee. I have never in all these years heard you go for it like that. It was so out of character. I couldn't believe my ears.'

'Oh I was just the worm turning, I s'pose. I just hope New Labour don't betray us. I mean Blair goes on about working and building a new Britain. What does he think I've been doing all my life? Working people know all about working. Work is what we *do*. Talk about teaching your grandmother to suck eggs!'

'I loved hearing about Greece, but that visit to Monaco... Like something from *Hello* magazine. It was all a bit in-yer-face, really. I could just hear Mum's voice, "I wonder if they wear their tiaras on the yacht?"' More laughter. 'We couldn't keep up with that.'

172

'Even the V&A'd be out of their depth with the D&Ds,' said Dee.

'You're not wrong. What about our measly bottle of plonk? I really pushed the boat out with that one, you know.'

'I couldn't believe it when I saw their wine rack. Full to bursting and all twice what you paid. Oh my Heavens.'

More laughter.

'What are we going to do? I couldn't cope with them coming to us!'

'I might just give the Horticultural Society a miss for a while.'

'Thank God for that.'

'Or Spider Grandmother, Lotte. Think of what Essie would say!'

When we arrived home, we lit some candles in our bedroom, and Dee put on our Joan Baez tape. Joan has a lot to answer for in our house. D'you know the one about Stephanie's room? The shadows on the hills beyond? We do. We know every shade of meaning in her music. It's not my style to talk about intimate details. I just can't, okay? But I'd hate you to think we were missing out on anything just because I said we were spinsters. Let me put it like this — if you go into our garden in the early morning, when the sun's coming up over the downs and the dew is glistening on a million spiders' webs, think of us, under the duvet, the previous night. While the spiders were spinning away in the bushes, we were loving one another.

I think of the spiders spinning now and it reminds me of the time when Dee, Gail and I listened to the legend of Spinsters' Rock. We brought back beautiful luminous pictures of the dolmen on Dartmoor, and we knew we had a book to spin yarns for. So where does the rock come into it?

The rock is the earth.

We spin and spin, enough tales to fill a dream garden. Every bramble has notice to quit and the weeds daren't come over the fence from the downs.

The rock is safety.

We have spun a safety net here, the three of us, me and Dee and our young companion, Gail. We uncovered the summer

173

house and created a safe haven for her. No one can take that away. It's important to weave a safety net for a young woman who has only bad dreams of the past.

The rock is the safety of the earth beneath our feet.

It is safe housing for women, not only women who are born into security, but the rest of us, who need it just as much. We need stability, because without it, we can't go on to make other dreams: to weave better lives for us all.

Esther
August, 1998

It's August in west Cornwall. There is summer sunshine and dazzling light on white surf. I live only a stone's throw from Zennor quoit, and it has become a significant place for me – my own Spinsters' Rock. Granite cliffs are solid beneath my feet, granite walls of my new home are around me. I am held safely in a new environment, where I spin my words. After hours of work I can rest to refresh myself, aware of the external world. I am close to the elements of earth, air, water and fire, but protected from them. I can see out but do not have to emerge until renewed and ready, like a newborn child emerging from a womb.

It's holiday time here, and flaming wild montbretia colours these cliffs and waysides with vermilion orange. Stooks and rolled bales are in the cornfields and everywhere there is the abundance of harvest.

In ancient times in this land, the harvest Goddesses were celebrated as the golden sun – She who ripens the crops; and the Lammas moon – She who hangs full and yellow over Her bountiful fields. In the village of Morvah, very near Hermit's Hut, there was great feasting, dancing and games, to celebrate the harvest every year.

I have found a new spirituality group here and am not as solitary as I was last winter. There are a dozen of us from the drumming group who celebrate the festivals together, though only six of us are lesbians. I have also met two local women, Lerryn and Tarn, who live together in Penzance, and are founder members of the women's tree planting and conservation group there. The politics of conservation, permaculture and the reforesting of this land have become important parts of my everyday life.

I enjoy being with the women and I feel that I am harvesting myself and my creativity now, in this lovely place.

I am alone at night and wake alone each morning. But I am not lonely. My years with Phoebe are behind me to sustain and nourish me. She and Isobel have not become lovers again, but are commencing a new journey – starting the long process of healing the rift. I am truly glad for them both that they can find a way through to a new friendship. The rebuilding of trust takes much time. Isobel holds the view that it's a mistake to try to reinvent relationships, and that you can never go back to how it once was, because you have changed so much in the meantime.

Meanwhile, in the women's group, we have been talking about the meaning of our politics and spirituality. We are trying to redefine the festivals to avoid having to link the Earth Mother with straight pagan concepts of consorts or sun gods, or the 'balance' of male and female energies. Those of us who are lesbians in the group feel that a women-only spirituality is essential for us. But some of the group have come from other traditions, so the political negotiations and discussions continue: and I find that the group is exciting and dynamic.

Over the Irish Sea, in a small town in rural Eire, the summer Goddess, Teiltu, opened her skirts and shed bounty on all her people. Her children loved her and revered her, dancing for her in the August sunshine. Her foster-son Lugh held a great feast for her on the first of August, every year. The place was Tell town; Teiltu's town.

There is still a feast there annually, with games and dancing, but the people of this century have forgotten the origin of the party, and they call their festival, and the month, Lughnasad, thinking only of Lugh and the great spectacle he held there. Their failure and ours to remember that it was held in honour of his mother has cast a shadow over her, as if every year, the neglect of her memory is like a minor eclipse.

There is a book here on the shelf at Hermit's Hut called *The Eclipse of the Sun*, by Janet McCrickard. She says that in ancient times the sun was loved and revered for her femaleness all over the world and throughout the year. Indeed, Teine, the word for fire, is a female word, and the largest fire we know of is the sun herself.

Here in Cornwall, the guide books tell me that fires were lit on holy hill tops for the summer solstice and a long chain of fires would stretch from the Isles of Scilly right up through the West Country as far as Glastonbury.

After the harvest, the sun moved to her time of equal day and equal night – the autumn equinox. Then the seasons turned towards Samhain, the time of the old woman, the wise one, she who waits at the crossroads. On Bodmin Moor the stone-age people built cairns along the crest of Caradon Hill so that they could mark the progress of the sun from cairn to cairn until Samhain.

So began the Celtic New Year from which festival the Old Grandmother, the Crone, known as the Cailleach, guided her people into the depth of winter and the long, dark nights. In the houses, in wintertime, the people would tell stories and gather round their firesides, forming their words with care, using story and song to describe the tribe, and give meaning and purpose to their lives. Winter was always a time for healing; a time for communality; a time for words. It was also a time for inner reflection, while the Earth Mother rested.

The days shortened imperceptibly, until finally the sun reached her lowest point and she stood still, waiting, resting. The Earth Mother's child was born as sunlight, and she showed herself in the first rays to re-emerge in the dawn of the winter solstice. Then people all over Europe would dance in a celebration of the return of the light. To the Romans she was Lucina, derived from Lusna of the Etruscans. On winter solstice morning young girls in Sweden still venture forth with candles in their hair, wearing crowns of light. Christianised, the Sun Goddess became St Lucy.

As the days lengthened the next festival was Imbolc – when the Cailleach became the young woman again – Bride, the triple Goddess of healing, poetry and smithcraft.

Then, with the commencement of springtime, there came a

festival of hope – vernal equinox. Rising and growing, the sun warmed the newly planted fields and, in the form of the spring Goddess Eostre, she gave her name to Easter, bringing the promise of summer bounties to come.

At Beltane, to mark the beginning of summer, the earth women were fertile. They lifted their skirts to expose their vulvas and jumped over the embers of the May Day fires to make themselves fruitful. They wore flowers in their hair and had a wicked lusty gleam in their eyes. The earth women became pregnant and anticipated harvest.

So the sun continued to rise, higher and higher in the sky, climbing to her zenith at midsummer, when our group went up to Mulfra quoit and watched as she danced in red and orange streamers of light. Then she came around to harvest, where I am now, harvesting my writing, my inner self, my solitude.

I am proud to be a spinster, and I have the annual cycle of light and dark for company.

I have been into the fields this week to collect corn, and have made a corn dolly for my mantel shelf. She embodies the spirit of the corn, and the hope I have in my heart now, a woman alone again and satisfied to be so. She will preside over my hearth this winter, over the open fire that's at the opposite end of my room from the Aga. She will bring sunlight into my autumn and wintertime, when I shall invite the women here into my home for storytelling.

In the spring next year, I shall carry her out into the garden, perhaps like the old times, with processions and singing, so that she can bless the earth; a symbol of sunlight, summer fruitfulness and plenty.

My writing continues, daily. The words flow like thread, the thread of life from inside me now. In my life my politics and creativity are being linked together, and the Earth Mother is centred inside me. There was an ache there for years, when I was mainly involved in politics. Something was missing and I am finding that additional something now – my soul.

I feel strangely connected with the scientists of the new physics

– in which everything is part of everything else. The stones, the soil, the sand, the trees, the animals, plants and birds, the ocean, the water molecules in the clouds and rain, the bones and blood of human bodies are all made of one and the same. The smaller the particles become, the more it reinforces my sense that we are all linked together and what we do affects everything else.

In this harvest time, the seeds of corn hold the secrets of next year's growth. So it is for me; the seeds of creativity and growth inside me are coming alive, and I am reconnected with every part of myself. I am part of the universe. The sun moves and I move with her, slowly or quickly, and everything changes. Even if I changed nothing about my life, my life would change because everything around me is in a constant state of flux.

I live without a man – so they call me a spinster.
I talk to Grandmother Moon – so they call me a lunatic.
I celebrate the Earth/and/Sun Mother – so they call me a
cackling witch.
I like my labels.

I am working, working, working on my writings, spinning my words, once again, into a warp thread strong enough to dance on.

Across the warp the pattern is a colourful weft of the closest of my women friends. Their names make a chant for me:

Phoebe, Laura, Nell and Lotte. Tracey, Dee and Gail.
Phoebe, Laura, Nell and Lotte. Tracey, Dee and Gail.

There are new friends too, from the Hermit's Hut trust and the tree planting, permaculture and conservation group.

And always Mum and Grammaclegg, who first taught me to knit, to work with yarn, to weave with women's friendship.

Deanne
September, 1998

I was always one for doing a lot of thinking. But I don't think in words, I think in pictures. So nowadays, if you ask me the meaning of time, I immediately think of Spinsters' Rock. That's its image in my mind. It's a time machine. It has three legs for past, present and future. It holds memories. It makes predictions. It shows me how time is transformed and yet simultaneously held.

Time seems to flow fast, and yet alongside this fast flow there is a slower stream, coming to us from other parts of the world, where there are other people in other cultures, linked with our lives in a million ways. These people are moving at a slower pace, and they understand that their ancestors watch over them.

I went to visit such a place recently, a far away island, that I would never have thought of going to but for my surrogate daughter, Isobel.

It was the island of Madagascar, and it was there that all the parts of my life came together, all the pieces of the puzzle. There I began, for the first time, to understand *time*. I am back home now, but part of my mind flies to and fro between here and Madagascar, where Isobel still lives and works, and where I found great peace and continuity. Nowadays in my life, I can think of past, present and future as one time, because all three are joined, here, in each moment, as if they were the three legs of Spinsters' Rock.

When I was a young woman there were times when I couldn't bear the present, because I was grieving for what was lost in the past and I was worried and uncertain of the future. Dora was in a mental hospital telling me that the colours of my paintings

180

seemed to be blurred, and Izzie was a little girl struggling to come to terms with being the only black child in a white south coast town.

However, in 1995, Isobel joined a team of engineers building wells on a UN project in Madagascar, and it was here that Lotte and I went for the holiday of a lifetime in the winter of 1996. It still seems like yesterday, so vivid do the pictures of it remain in my mind.

It is a very poor country, listed as the fourth or fifth poorest place in the world. The people still hold many traditional beliefs in ancestral powers. It is also a spectacularly beautiful island, where the animals and plants have evolved separately from the species on mainland Africa into distinct species such as lemurs, chameleons and zebu.

The visit was Isobel's gift to me, but when she asked if I would like to bring Lotte, who paid for herself by working overtime, I was very glad.

So, we flew in over the high plateau to Tana, the capital, and there was Isobel to meet me, smiling as ever, and with a little grey in her hair at the age of forty-four. With her was her new partner, Noross, whose warmth and friendliness made our whole visit easy and relaxed.

Noross was born and raised in Madagascar. She went to Paris and London to study medicine, then returned home to specialise in eye diseases. She also became involved in a campaign to conserve traditional Malagasy medicines. The people are so poor that they have begun to grow rice, but the growth causes some soil erosion. This has resulted in the loss of traditional plants; a loss which has been worsened by rapid deforestation of areas which are home to many of Madagascar's rare healing plants.

But we learned a lot about our part as westerners too. The best example I can think of is a little plant called the rosy periwinkle. Here in the west, it saves the lives of children with leukaemia, but not one penny goes back to Madagascar where the people cannot afford the medicines they need. Everywhere there is serious vitamin A deficiency and many of the children have vitamin A blindness. Even when the peasant farmers grow foods rich in vitamin A, such as carrots, they cannot afford to let their children eat them.

From Noross we learned that many village people suffered from serious cataracts. There were older men and women who hadn't seen their families for years and years. Family, tradition and continuity are everything to the Malagasy people, because of their ancestral beliefs. Noross was able to perform the cataract operations and was witness to their joy at being able to see their children and grandchildren again.

Our visit had a poignancy which was real and very new to me. After the facilities we took for granted at Mere Cottage and the expectations of our B&B guests, I felt completely changed by the presence of so many beggars in the street, and by meeting villagers in the remote rural areas who had never seen electricity. In a few places the children had never seen a white person. Probably no great loss! But we weren't called white, for it's a term of abuse. We were the vazaha – the foreigners.

It was a glorious four weeks, during which we saw the petrified forests of the west coast, and the rice fields of the east. Sometimes we travelled by horsedrawn cart, for in some areas horses are the only transport. We also walked for days, along hillsides where there were no roads. We ate local food; absorbed the colours of mimosas, the scent of frangipani; and heard the sounds of the wind on the terraced hillsides of maize, cassava and pineapples. We lay on long sweeping beaches as the Pacific ocean rolled towards this massive island which has only been populated for the past two thousand years.

We talked and talked, drank and ate, rested and relaxed. We explained to Izzie and Nor how it was that we had become a lesbian family again, now spanning three generations, and showed them our photos of Alicia and her friends running around the house and garden.

Izzie laughed happily. 'It lets me right off the hook. Though I'm too old even to contemplate children now. You were never going to be a lesbian granny through me, were you Dee? I always knew it wasn't for me. I wanted my work and I knew that it would fill all my waking hours.'

'What she says is more than true,' said Nor. 'I have to kidnap her to get any time to ourselves.'

'I'm a workaholic, I freely admit it.'

I smiled. 'It's such a treat having Gail and Sara and the children around. Makes me think about continuity. That's what it gives to me. We didn't plan it. You couldn't, could you? But we love it.'

Izzie said, 'Besides, being a granny is very different from being a single parent, eh Dee, because you can hand them all back at the end of it.'

Much laughter. I said, 'You're not wrong. The silence when they've gone . . . it descends like a quiet mist. Absolute bliss.'

'Also, it's a different world for the three children growing up in England now. As black children they're not on their own. Not like I was. There are others to help them deal with the racism.'

'That's right. It's still there of course, but they have more resources around them now, compared to you in Coombebury, love.'

Nor came in with, 'Izzie tells me tales from her childhood, the only black child in a white town. So different from my own. There were many of us, eight in our family. The rooms were small. Sometimes I'd fantasise about having my own space. But never to be without other children.' She reached for Isobel's hand and squeezed it.

Isobel said, 'We did well, didn't we, Dee? It couldn't have been easy for you when I burst out with, "Why did my mummy make me brown? You're not brown. I hate you Dee."' She stopped speaking, and we looked into one another's eyes, with rueful smiles. She continued, 'Many women in your situation would've sent me to social services and that'd have been the end of it. I could've been passed about like a parcel, from one foster home to another. You taught me compassion, Dee. I had to learn what it was like from your position, as well as my own.'

'We both did. You were very brave in that school. Remember when Raymond Phelps was bullying you, and I had to face up to Mrs Phelps? I'll never forget teaching you to fight back. *Having* to teach you to fight. But they never got you after that did they, love?'

'Certainly not. You never forget those early childhood lessons. You get to know how strong you are. If you want to survive in a white world, that is. And now I'm working here, and I've met Nor. There is love in my life again. We work very hard here. So I've been longing for this break, you know. When you said yes you could get a month off, and Gail'd take care of Mere Cottage, I was overjoyed. We simply cannot get to Britain for the foreseeable future, and for you to come here is wonderful.' She paused, smiling, then added, 'Tell us about Sara's Welsh family. How are they coming to terms with not having Alicia?'

'It was hard for them. They were grief stricken when Alicia moved to Brighton. Angry. Distressed. But then they came to see Sara's house, and they met Sara's friend, Nadine. That was the turning point. They realised that Sara had put a lot of thought into it and that Alicia had the other two little ones to play with. But they did give Sara a hard time. She still isn't out to them. Nadine is very straight, so no hints in that direction, nothing to alert them. They still don't know that Gail is Sara's lover.'

'How is Gail?'

'She's very happy. She accepts Sara's situation. Says it has to be Sara's timing.'

Lotte added, 'Gail has a big thing about Sara not losing her parents over this. It's understandable really.'

I said, 'And Alicia is a lively, happy seven-year-old. She's going fine at school. Naturally, Sara's parents think she'd be better off in Cardiff, but she's Sara's child. Sara knows her own mind.'

'That's the main thing then – you have to know what you want before you can try and get it. We can't possibly be 'out' here. People know that we share our house, but that's as far as it goes. Hopefully, they think of us as a scientist and a medic, getting on with the job.'

'Is it lonely?'

'Yes and no. We both love our work don't we, Nor?'

'That's right Izzie. That's absolutely right. I was alone here, apart from my family connections. I loved my work but there was no one special in my life. I wasn't searching for anyone. I knew who I was, but the work was completely absorbing. That is what we both understand. I could've stayed in Paris, or London. Been 'out', found someone. Much easier life. Money, success. But I wanted and needed to come home. I was quite prepared to be on my own here. I'd made a decision. Then you came into my life and now I have everything.'

Isobel grinned.

To see Isobel so happy made my heart joyful. Yes, she and Phoebe had both flown to Harare to meet one another, but Isobel had been through such a long separation from Phoebe and she was determined not to get drawn back in. I think that is part of the reason she moved to Madagascar. To go forward in life, not to run away, but not to look backwards either.

So we travelled onwards, visiting the Tsingy limestone areas, and we, Lotte and I, could observe from how she looked, how she talked, how she lived, that Isobel had found a wonderful partner and, amid all her changes, some emotional security at last.

She had fallen in love with an island, then met one of the island's most prestigious daughters. Black like herself, their affection and respect for one another shone like mirrors for us to gaze into and see our own relationship reflected back. That holiday was one of the happiest times of my whole life. Completion, continuity, contentment.

We weren't there at the time of the Malagasy New Year, which is called Alahamady. I was rather glad. The festival is one of delight in the ancestors, when they are taken bodily from the tombs and rewrapped in woven lambas – special cloths for sacred remembrance. They are carried through the streets with dancing and feasting, before being replaced, and rededicated again. Not my kind of thing.

But it put me in mind of the stone-age people who built Spinsters' Rock, for that was used as a burial chamber, for the ashes of the dead. In all seasons, all weather, and at all times, people would come to visit the sacred place. They would have asked their ancestors for guidance, comfort, help and protection. There was no gap between the dead and the living. Time did not mean separation.

So it is in my life, in my daughter's life, Lotte's life – and so it is in Dora's life and death. I think that perhaps without my visit to Madagascar I might not have made the link, realised the connection. It is Esther who says we are all part of everything and whatever we do affects everything else. I still have my eyesight and can still see the wonders of the Tsingy and the petrified forests of Madagascar. I can see, if I need to, the dolmen on Dartmoor. But more than that I now understand that in some parts of the world people are so poor they cannot afford to eat the carrots they grow and become blind as a result. But they can still see their ancestors. Seeing is not believing. Knowing is believing. It has nothing to do with eyes.

I don't think of spirituality as Esther does. I don't want or need to. We are very different women on very different life journeys. But we are part of everything, and therefore linked. We are not biological sisters but I am lovers with her sister and we have become sisters through friendship. Just like me and Nell. Lotte calls this web weaving. I am content with that.

I think of Dora every day. She is part of me and always will be. I can still see the huge blocks of colour that we made from flowers at her funeral. I hope she understood and felt the love that was in all that colour. I hope she rests in peace. I don't want to have her bones disinterred and rewrapped in a lamba, but if I did, it would be made of bright blocks of colour.

I think back through the years to Penny Acre Farm where it all began. Poor as we were in the Second World War, we often had carrots to eat. We are Europeans now, although there is, as I speak, war in some parts of Europe. There is war all over the world. It shifts its arena from time to time. My wish for the future is an end to war; a new era in which there is no hungry child, no parent despairing, no grandmother with cataracts due to poverty, no child unloved, and no single mother without food, water, shelter, health and education.

The capstone of the rock is *this* moment in time. *Now*. Now, I understand it. I stand under it. Look up at the capstone from underneath. Now is the time to speak, to change, to move forward. In my life, the women are very strong. We have had to be. We shall have to be. There is so much to do.

The sun is rising and the work is not yet done.

There are boulders to carry, ropes to pull, voices to raise, and capstones to lift.

The time is now. We have dolmens to build, before breakfast.